THE RIVER RUNS:
STORIES
BY THOMAS RAY GARCIA

Prickly Pear Publishing & Nopalli Press

Santa Fe, New Mexico

PRICKLY PEAR PUBLISHING

Publishing Acknowledgements: "Seventh Man" was originally published in
riverSedge in 2016, and it co-won the Fiction Prize.

"La Lomita" was originally published as "Ghostlights" in *figments* in 2015, and it won
the Flash Fiction Prize from *The New Engagement* in 2017.

"The Curandera on Alameda Street" was originally published in *BorderSenses* in
2016, and it won the Princeton University Ward Mathis Prize in 2016.

"Burn The Sun" was originally published in *The New Engagement*'s inaugural print
issue in 2017.

Winner of the 2022 Américo Paredes Literary Arts Prize for Fiction sponsored by
FlowerSong Press and Prickly Pear Publishing.

First Edition, Printed in the United States of America

Library of Congress Control Number: 2023933991

Garcia, Thomas Ray

The River Runs: Stories by Thomas Ray Garcia— 1st Prickly Pear Publishing ed.
/Thomas Ray Garcia

ISBN 978-1-889568-21-8 (pbk.)

I. Title.

Fiction, Family, Code Switching, Coming of Age, Southern Border, Texas, Northern
Mexico, Rio Grande Valley.

ACKNOWLEDGEMENTS

Thank you, Lina Diaz, for designing the cover of this book.
Her work can be found at cgdillustrart.wixsite.com/cpcc

Thank you, Max Lozano, Isaac Bailon, and Aurelio Montemayor,
for reading early drafts of these stories and supporting
this volume's development since 2015.

TABLE OF CONTENTS

SEVENTH MAN

The boys and I used to run all over the Rio Grande Valley like Road Kings until the seventh man taught me what it meant to roam. There we were, half naked and sweating even before the sun rose above the flatland horizon, sneaking under tollbooth gates and over chained fences until we entered the Santa Ana Wildlife Refuge. Although it was an hour until opening, who would kick out six cross country runners cutting across trails and roads and brush lands? And if we were caught, that middle-aged, mafia-hat-wearing, goatee uneven and gray bastard of a coach would do anything to bail out his job security — we all helped each other out that way.

Even in the twilight I admired my hodgepodge of a team. Who could forget Beans' telenovela celebrity chin, scarred from his monthly trips across the river? And Russian, who was as white as you could get, was probably more Mexican than all of us combined, but he was pale and his middle name was "Ivan," and that was all that mattered to Coach Austin while bestowing his nicknames. And then there was Danny Bear, the darkest runner Coach Austin has ever had, and so his nickname followed suit. Julian and Josh, keeping their real names because they transcended the nickname game, were the two self-appointed team leaders and traitors to that necessary tranquility before a run; they ran ahead without telling anyone else. Only Russian and I had Garmins, and this sole fact made us saviors, so we caught up in haste.

"Too fast," Russian said under a mutter. Those two words slowed us down.

And who wants to rush past the Santa Ana scenery with its cracked soil and suffocating paths winding past one another, a road here and a trail there, all leading in circles until our twelve miles were over and we returned home with nothing to do but wait until the next run? In the middle of a heartbeat, we sunk into a rhythm led by shoes three hundred miles over-worn.

"Russian, let's go sub-six on the last mile or what?" Danny Bear asked.

No reply, only breathing, and so Danny Bear acted: A jerk to the right to escape the pack, and then a surge forward to interrupt Russian's stride. No good, for the pack sided with Russian, and we answered Danny Bear's treason by turning into a clearing off the main trail.

After a silent minute, Danny Bear caught the back end with Beans, Julian and Josh remained in the middle, and Russian and I led the pack with a tinge of reluctance since both of us were beat after a long week of studying English and Biology and whatever else we thought would help us escape this never-ending run. How many miles now? My Garmin sounded off in reply: One. One out of twelve, twelve out of sixty-five or sixty-six that week. We were only sixteen years old and there were only six of us. We were like the Spartans of the Southmost South, where the weight of Texas crushes the upheaving Mexico and we're caught in the middle trying to hold one up and push the other down.

If only I had known the struggle going on in their minds at that moment. Whether they realized it or not, they wanted to escape. Their futures foretold it: Russian with his unfulfilled PhD dreams and Julian — the MIT bright-child of Pharr or Donna or whatever town he put down on the school form, who threw out his back and joined a frat and fell in love with a brunette back home — who left Texas and came back to Texas and never went anywhere but Texas. For love, he said. For fear, I said. Josh joined the Border Patrol (told you he was a traitor) while Danny Bear disappeared into who knows where — maybe some obscure mechanic shop down by Las Milpas — I probably drive past him every day. And Beans? He overdosed the night after graduation.

We all yearned for that salvation from our duties as citizens of the Rio Grande Valley and my words fail to capture the wheel we ran inside every day until I left and "became a writer like Jack London" like my dreams told me I would. And I still run (six days a week in fact) to fulfill my duty but to jump so far ahead of my story would do injustice to the immediacy of the moment — we were six runners then. Six was actually an odd number. This revelation struck me as I fell back with Beans and Danny Bear and watched as we stomped our souls into the dead earth. I saw ten soleless shoes rising and falling in unison, then discordant, then both, and then I stopped staring at the legs and looked at the bare backs. Josh must have been whipped by his abuelo last night. Russian with his acned back didn't mind, neither did Julian with his suntanned, blotched, bronze shoulders pumping him forward. I fell into Beans' rhythm, a steady pace, relaxed with the world, not resisting the inevitable. Danny Bear followed.

"Who's gonna be our seventh man?" I asked, tired of the silence. "We can't compete without him. Ricky, Gecko, or Takis?"

"Se mamón Tommy," Beans said. "Focus on yourself."

That's the way it was in the Rio Grande Valley. I remembered joining the team as an overweight, idealistic cheerleader spouting spirit and teamwork and goodwill to those who would take it. But no one did; we ran as a pack but lived in our minds. We woke up before our parents rose and ran before the sun rose and showered naked (hiding our roses) and learned how not to learn and ran again after the sun set; we were miserable but reassured in our cycle of sleep, run, school, run, sleep. And here we were, at the edge of the nation, running away from it all, together but separated by that invisible border of human disconnection. The loneliness of the long-distance runner was real.

The sun remembered to rise by mile four, and all attempts at connection were replaced by the gasping of humid air. We were lost. Even if Beans knew the routes, he refused to pick up the pace and lead the pack, so we ran through trails overlapping and never-ending. Thickets surrounded us, but I could still make out the breaks in the trees and bushes to where the river rushed by. I could hear it gurgling. I'd never seen the river, but it was right there. Momma told me to stay away from it. But it's beyond the trees and right there, separating two worlds, bleeding with foreign blood, and I was the only one who was thinking this as we turned into a new trail, the Bobcat Trail of all names, and we left behind the wonder of that false placidity with no reflection whatsoever.

I had it. I ran past them all. No one protested as I swung my arms in a frenzy brought on by delusions of my rut. Their route was now my whim, and they struggled to follow me as I circled back toward treaded paths and unfamiliar branches glowing with light. And there was the river, calm and turquoise, no hints of life anywhere, hidden by branches and bent-over trees that seemed to return to the land. I stopped. My chest heaved in tune with my mind, pulsing with adrenaline, and I felt like crossing the Rio Grande and disappearing into nowhere.

"If you're tired, then don't pick up the pace," Julian said, annoyed.

I turned to face him, but in my rush my eyes caught a shirt thrown across a nearby trunk. I approached it. It was wet.

5

"Watch out for beaners," Josh said.

Only Russian joined me in retracing soft spots in the soil toward the incline leading out of the river, and then following the traces of footprints that were separated by two-foot-long strides. Bursting into a sprint, I ignored the protests behind me, my eyes on the trail, discovering candy boxes and empty prescription bottles until they stopped appearing and I was at a loss until I saw him.

A tall, shirtless teen with a thick bigote stood hunched over, hiding the scar across his chest. His shorts revealed his darkened thighs, not unaccustomed to sunlight. His calf muscles tightened as if in constant alertness, ready to flee, but he remained staring absently at the six sweaty bodies circled together facing him, the beat stranger.

"Pinche Tommy," Beans said. Our breathing had subsided. The four miles, and all the miles we had run, meant nothing standing face-to-face with a true lonesome traveler.

After a light tap on my shoulder, Julian ran back through the woods. The pack followed him. I too followed, shocked at the nonchalant encounter until I realized he was following us; he ran, long legs pushing off the same ground we tread, keeping a considerable distance away but still maintaining a pace only conditioned runners could match. Julian and the others had dashed away, pretending they saw nothing, and let the dust left by their soles remain as the only evidence they had seen the teen that now neared us, gaining momentum without a sweat, determined to join this solitary band of runners.

I slowed my pace, waiting for him to catch up. What was there to fear? Would he attack me, steal the shorts and shoes that belonged to the school, run far and away until he was me and I was dead?

But he just laughed. He exaggerated his arm movements, contorted his face so his lips pushed forward, and his eyes widened. Then he stopped goofing, and then he started up again, never breaking his gaze with me.

"Want to run with us?" I asked. A naïve hope had kindled in me, and despite the improbability of it all, I hoped he would say yes. No reply. He just pushed forward, looking back as if expecting me to respond in turn, and I did, extending my stride and quickening my pace until our legs chugged in a silent harmony disturbed only by our breathing.

The pack lay ahead. From afar I noticed how they composed a morphing vehicle of bodies that worked separately for a common good, that is, a physical reminder of human existence that many take for granted but its absence can easily de-motivate the long-distance runner stuck in the never-ending step, step, breathe, step, step, breathe cycle that both prolongs and invites suffering. And here I shared this experience with the teen beside me, matching my movements limb by limb, never daring to move ahead or shrink back, content with his position.

I asked myself why the long-distance runner never questions why, but always asks how things happen or how things will end up, until the teen suddenly sprinted forward, catching up with the pack. Russian and Julian and Josh and Danny Bear and Beans ran on. They knew, or maybe they really didn't know, about the seventh man in their midst; a new breathing pattern and running gait had to have registered in their subconscious, sharpened only by miles of thoughtlessness, but I realized that it didn't matter whether they thought the teen was he or me. He could run with the pack if he could keep up with the pack, and that was that.

How he could run like that after trekking who knows how many miles and living off scraps and swimming across that river I will never know, but I did know he wanted to be one with the pack of runners that provided anonymity, protection, and freedom despite none of us offering any of these things.

Of course, I didn't arrive at this conclusion until we ran alongside the scenic road and passed a trolley full of workers and visitors reveling in its shade, and out of the corner of my eye I saw a transformation in the teen's face: It was done, it was over, the journey had ended, and it was time to go home; I knew this because those eyes betrayed all traces of fear. He held his breath mid-stride. But the trolley passed. Only waves from tourists had graced our group of seven runners, all apparently coming from the same place and going to the same place, all one entity in the eyes of a stranger. The teen's shoulders eased.

We turned off the road and into a path that ran along a dried-up lake. Its red soil cooked in the heat, as did our bodies as we silently yearned for water and relief from the remaining three miles. Where we were headed, I had no idea, and this fact bothered me until a swell of anger rushed from my head to my feet and I ran up to the front with Russian and Julian, dominant in my ambitions to take control of this lost vehicle. The teen must have felt the same, for he joined me, and I remained quiet until the urge not to ask was overcome by my curiosity.

"¿Cómo te llamas?" I asked between breaths.

"Jesse," he said. And that was all he ever said.

So Jesse and I took the lead, Russian and Julian following, Danny Bear and Josh straggling behind, and Beans behind them ensuring we stay together, yet this was the last thought on the rest of our minds as all we thought was run, run, run, don't look back, just move on, go past that tree over there that looks burnt from the South Texas sun and jump over that fallen branch and watch out for that dip in the trail and don't stop.

My Garmin beeped mile ten, and against the wall I went, feeling a growing heaviness in my legs and fatigue burning my chest. Everything slowed down, from the birds crisscrossing the laneless sky and the leaves drooping down, and I even blinked and breathed slower, believing the whole world had joined me in my madness until I looked over to Jesse who ran straight and tall and confident, those lean arms swaying in rhythmic motion, hypnotic to someone as exhausted as me, and I couldn't help letting him gain distance on me so I could watch that body defy time, motion, and the stifling existence we all suffered.

The pack stayed with me, I was the new leader, but Jesse was the true alpha, running at least fifty meters ahead, directing our path on his impulse. I questioned none of it. I followed blindly, his movements inspiring my own, knowing that I couldn't quit, and despite the quickening pace I refused to look down at my Garmin to know how many minutes were left because I didn't want it to be over.

If I had known how it would all go after this run and all our other runs, I would have said don't bury your nose in the books Russian, it's all worthless, go find your voice like Julian except he found love instead and not even in Cambridge but right under his shoe here in the lowland Rio Grande. And Beans? Don't die Beans. Go work with Danny Bear, go make that engine scream, go follow Josh with his forlorn crossers. Remember the miles, remember them all, and although we will never run together again, my words will never let your spirits die.

In the final moments of that run, the pack surrounded me like before, but it felt like never before. I was propelled forward by an unexplainable force from the energy emanating from their muscles and mouths. We were six, but we were one, yet we were six minds six souls twelve legs that pushed beyond the limits that the world placed on us; we infiltrated this refuge, we ran the miles the way we wanted to run them, we found someone as lost as ourselves and we followed him, he who had transcended it all, and we thought nothing.

I extended my stride to catch up to Jesse, and in this impossible task I found myself smiling, chasing after a long-forgotten desire I thought I had lost somewhere along the way. I laughed like a child.

The trees and trails looked familiar again, and a sign marked the beginning of the Malachite Trail up ahead. The fence appeared in the distance, and as we slowed down Jesse sped on, heaving his whole body onto the wire, until he climbed up and out and ran past Coach Austin's mini-van and toward the rest of Texas.

"Who was that?" Coach Austin asked us while we climbed over.

"Jesse," I said.

"He can run." And that's all that he ever said about that day.

Now, whenever I wake up early enough to see the sun rise over the Rio Grande Valley and spot a long-distance runner hiding in its shadows, in his eyes all that road behind and beyond him suddenly gone as if my gaze could pierce kneecaps and pick his soul out and deport his dreams, I remember Jesse, who could have been Jesus for all we knew, and I look the other way.

(2015)

PROSPERERS

Ariel knew the knowing look. She had seen it on the faces of her father who scoffed at her Manhattan dance dreams, her boss who hired her underaged and undocumented, and her pastor who began his sermons by denouncing Buddhist babies from Japan. But now Pastor Meyer redirected his Biblical wrath toward strip clubs. On the evening of Ariel's graduation. In front of everyone's parents. And before her next shift at the Caballero Club.

The chapel adjoined to Faith Christian School resounded with Amens, each affirmation enlarging Pastor Meyer's sweat spots. Deprived of air conditioning, his audience felt the brush of his spirit bounding past them toward an unseen, lost soul in the back. Enraptured, no one turned around to discover who. Talking, talking, Pastor Meyer gazed past the two-dozen heads, each word of worship revving his grace-inspired movements until he executed his signature move: pulling out his black wallet to demonstrate God's beatitude. The palm is His love, the wallet the soul, the contents inside eternal sin.

"Yes, a mere expressway separates us from that sinful place," he said, fingering the barren flaps. "Let me ask you: If we expend sin, are we owed forgiveness from our Father?"

The stunt amazed Ariel, who didn't know how Pastor Meyer's wallet could be empty after collecting her back-pay tuition, nor why he was sermonizing on her part-time job. She remembered the weekday midnights where stiletto clicks signaled her presence, lights illuminated her brown skin with a rainbow hue, and borderlands insanities drove men with memories and bills to burn to her. From spectacle on the stage to lady on their laps, she had released her body to countless hands. Her only body, yet so many hands. And there Pastor Meyer stood, his roaming eyes returning to her at the end of every declaration, knowing.

Shivering, Ariel broke his gaze, regaining control of the spinning compass in her head. She returned to her body, sitting alone next to her empty guest seat, and imagined what her father could be doing now. Eyes sunken into a mad reverie playing inside his broken brain. Holes hidden in the neck flab, insulin syringes hidden in the carpet, and everything else the doctors didn't diagnose coughed up in phlegm. Brownness blanketing him as he slept through afternoons and evenings on the living room couch with telenovelas blaring in the background. Whenever the city shut off the lights, he lay awake and absent, too numb to notice his daughter's escapades and early morning returns. In these instances of poverty-induced silence, even the slightest taps from Ariel's dancing feet would elicit a "¡Cállate!"

There were no East Coast odysseys in her father's visions of tomorrow, only what was on the channel guide. Their bodies were intertwined, but hers was on the line while his was in decline.

Yet every other Wednesday he would rise with spirited praise and drive to the all-men's Bible Study with Pastor Meyer, who orchestrated the circle of jerks. Or, as they called themselves, "The Prosperers," the only information Ariel was supposed to know.

"Prosperers adhere," her father would say to her after each meeting. "Get to God, Ariel. Prosperers adhere."

Of all the bastardized words the English language inserted into her father's mind, "prosperers" adhered. "Live prosperers and take the Father's hand," read the misspelled marque outside of Faith Christian School five years prior, which led to Ariel's enrollment. Completing those Accelerated Christian Education workbooks and scribbling in every key word ingrained into her brain — faith, redemption, prosperity — had taught her that the Earth spun on spirit energy, King James wrote the Bible in 1607, and school tuition was like taxes except it went to God. In his sickness, her father clung to his mantra, even after the welfare checks ran dry and Ariel learned that she was learning nothing. He believed they were "prosperers," and that was all that mattered.

As she sat in the chapel, Ariel waited for the word to burst forth from Pastor Meyer's mouth, but he shoved his wallet into his pocket instead. Wait for the diploma, she reassured herself. You may have no documents, but that diploma is the only paper you need to move on. Those public-school teachers might have flunked you for speaking Spanish too often, but God is good. Trust Him, not him.

"So, without further delay, let us Amen to our first graduating class as they make their way to the stage," he said. His vibrato rumbled with sacred self-importance not unfamiliar to the congregation, who welcomed his command combining the holy with the mundane.

But it was the new voice infiltrating the chapel that caught Ariel off guard. She heard its solemn serenity, sensing the voice's strange familiarity as it mispronounced the chant "a man." As she assumed the third, and last, spot in line behind the lunch-lady's daughter and the principal's son, she peaked past the intermittent camera flashes resembling the rush of strobe lights in the club, where they had shielded her from patrons not much younger than her father. Here, she half-hoped they would come from her father.

"One more time: An Amen for God's children!"

"Amen."

The voice sounded again, and Ariel froze. Her boss leaned on the exit door at the back of the chapel. She shut her eyes. Mr. Morales' face disappeared. But then it would reappear, as if in and out of her memory, which also housed the repressed gropes and catcalls impelling her to roam the club trancelike and robotic until his next demand.

Then the chapel fell away, and she saw Mr. Morales slumping in his reclining chair in the middle of his office. His bloated stomach allowed him to rest a Corona on its cusp as he gazed at the women plastered on his walls. Paperwork was strewn on one side of the desk, but orderly and stacked on the other, and his prized, framed portrait with Selena Quintanilla leaned on one corner.

"Yeah, I know I'm out in August. What else do you want?" Ariel had asked. "Your face is hiding something."

"Meyer talked to your dad about it."

Ariel felt an invisible weight crush her chest.

"Nah, nah, I mean about the graduation ceremony," Mr. Morales said as he pulled a post-it note-covered Bible out of his drawer and dropped it on his desk. "Last Prosperers meeting of the school year. All business."

"What did dad say?"

"He's proud of you."

"How did he say it?"

"He thinks you're a damn grocer at H-E-B! He's proud you make the bed sometimes. Ask him yourself. I'm already breaking meeting code, here."

She imagined her father slouching before the television, watching immigrants cross the border on the news. River water still slushing in his head from his last crossing. All her words just Rio

Grande sounds. No breathing until the scene changed. She would wonder, but never ask what had happened. She imagined he didn't know either.

"Look, I've kept it on the downlow. I don't even know you," Mr. Morales said.

"Yeah, I wish," Ariel said. "I'm looking forward to getting that diploma so I can make more paper somewhere else, like New York. I don't know, but I'll get there somehow on my own."

"Well, that's the thing. It's not a golden triangle without Meyer and me."

He had slurred the sentence, and perceiving his slipping supremacy, he racked the ring on his middle finger against the wood, each sound louder than before. But it was too late. Ariel smirked, remembering how he sweated while confirming her measurements for the second time. She walked up to the desk, towering above him slumped over in his chair. She knew men risked their lives to watch underage girls dance, which kept Mr. Morales in business, which paid her debts, which kept Meyer afloat. In his eyes was the recognition that she depended on him as much as he depended on her.

"OK, OK. Meyer also told me something after the meeting," Mr. Morales said, clearing his throat. "Look, even after you graduate, Meyer needs to get a cut of your stage fees and tip outs, or else he's not gonna stay quiet."

Ariel laughed as she pictured Pastor Meyer attempting to threaten him. Pastor Meyer's clumsy hands jerking open his wallet and Mr. Morales folding the bills inside. Pastor Meyer patting Mr. Morales on the back and reciting a verse before handing him a beer. It was pathetic, but it was her foundation.

"I don't care whether he reports you. I'm graduating. I can get a real job anywhere soon."

"No, I mean stay quiet to your dad, mija."

A shiver rippled across Ariel's arms, followed by a hardening shudder that crept throughout her body. "Why? Is this blackmail? Is that what he's doing?"

"Look, you know he's an Old Testament bastard. And you know I'm a follower of Jesus. But I'm also a businessman, a negotiator. So, just listen to me and he'll keep quiet."

Black fingernails clawed into Ariel's neck, tearing into the invisible authority that choked her. No wheedling, no concessions, just silence, and she stared into Mr. Morales' weary pupils as he winked consecutively and unsuccessfully, as he did after all his negotiations ranging from elote sales to pulga deals.

"Sounds like I should have some say in it, then."

Mr. Morales wheezed, spilling beer and blowing paperwork onto the floor in a wild Chicano style that imbued his waning health with strength he knew didn't exist. Then a grin crinkled against his wrinkling fore-lip. His tongue slid across his chin, sapping sweat.

"Look, tough girl. Your dad needs your cash. Meyer needs your cash. This place gives you your cash. Why?" he asked himself. "Because your dad and Meyer are the base. I'm the top of the triangle. We all depend on one another, even when we don't realize it. Prosperers adhere."

Ariel frowned with lips curved like the railroad tracks derailing the runaway train of her teenage years and exited the office. She felt him guessing at something hidden beneath her outfit as she glided across the floor and onto the stage, dreaming of home — while the boom shaking the room rung on the chrome pole as she swung to the rhythm of radio waves and flashes of light over faces lust-filled and lonely. To avoid his leers, she would spin around and around in a chaotic zoom, her vision blurred, rushing everywhere yet always returning to the blank face painted onto the mirror, watching her moves. In that reflection she could see the only true escape from the endless shifts colliding into one another day and night, week to week, in a snapshot reel measured by her thinning, hungry waist. To the gawkers and gropers, she was another body, but it was always Ariel standing inside the mirror.

Now there was no mirror, and Ariel appeared lost mid-stride on the chapel stage. Amid her confusion, she found Pastor Meyer, standing expectant like a cynical guardian angel blocking the stairwell. His glare seemed to penetrate her mind. He saw the accursed club, mirrored from wall to floor, with the dance stage glowing phosphorescent and sexy pink. He saw her flipping, swirling, rolling from one edge to the other, mesmerizing on her own but made irresistible with the music that thumped the ground and shook the tequila glasses. He saw her body toned and starved and Chicana entrancing men who purchased her empowerment for their pleasure, all a drunken dumb-show full of language barriers and erections. And all he had to give her was a big rock.

"Where the fuck is the paper?" Ariel said under her breath.

When she stopped before Pastor Meyer, he handed her the stone. Seven years attending the school, each grade level an exercise in eye rolling, had dulled Ariel's New York dreams — and yet those dreams became undone as she accepted the stone. It sat in her hands, weighing down any freedom she could imagine.

"God is our Father, our rock. Rest on him and you will stand tall. The world is your mission," Pastor Meyer said. "God bless you."

"Blessed be he who gives me my diploma," Ariel said, stuck between sarcasm and inquiry, gripping her stone as if it held the answers. Pastor Meyer rushed toward the podium. She trudged past hoots and whistles from the church-founders, permanent Winter Texans to the untrained eye, and returned to her seat.

"As we bid farewell to our graduating seniors this evening, we must remember that we should be one with the world but abstain from tainting it with sin. Have a blessed day. Amen."

"Amen."

Darting her eyes toward the back of the chapel, Ariel dodged the small talkers reaching out their hands, but Mr. Morales no longer stood against the back wall. In between the departing families, she spotted Pastor Meyer peering past shoulders and heads to where she stood. She twisted in place, maneuvered around the chairs, and escaped through the narrow door.

The springtime South Texas heatwaves washed over her robe. The warmth chilled her out, heat inhaling mirages out of her mind and blowing them onto the pavement: Visions of coins wrapped with pesos organized on her mattress. Three-dollars-a-day sandwiches from the street-corner tienda. Faded outfits dirtied from fingers sullied and sweaty. But one real image was Mr. Morales leaning against Pastor Meyer's white truck. As if handprints had arisen on her skin, Ariel crossed her arms, shielding herself from the glaring penetration of the knowing look. That was the one thing Faith and Caballero had in common: bald men with that look.

She delayed her walk. It was easy to forget herself when she danced, feeling in and out of the room all the same, but she would not now. She could not. The push and pull of her boss, her pastor, her father was impossible to navigate without a body. It was all she had left. With that in mind, she walked as if on a tightrope. On Mr. Morales' face was stained a peculiar middle-aged sense of urgency, hardened by a silent, moving mouth. What words were uttered in the moments before their encounter Ariel could never guess, but after months of daydreaming about father death blues, she remembered sitting with legs crisscrossed on Mr. Morales' lap time after time after time, and she decided she could serve no more.

"Is this a game to you?" she asked, looking back at the growing crowds. "Get out of here before I kill you."

"All right, Cain and Abel. Calm down. Look, he's lost it. The books aren't looking good. Enrollment's down already for next year."

"You think it has something to do with giving out rocks instead of diplomas?"

"Look, the school isn't accredited. Even I thought it was. Someone leaked all this about the rocks, and it had to be one of the men from our Prosperers meeting because Meyer only trusts these guys. Now parents want their kids out. Meyer feels like it's all a set-up."

"Was it you?"

"Why the hell? It's over, Ariel. It's over for everyone. I came to tell you so you can save your ass before he does some shit like call ICE."

The noose had fallen, but a tightening sensation enveloped Ariel's skull and crept down her throat full of gone words until a single word broke through.

"ICE?"

"Look, forget I said that. Truth is, Meyer thinks he's the victim," Mr. Morales said as he pulled a set of keys out of his pocket.

"He's in a corner and lashing out. I'm shutting down and getting out of here before he bites. You need to confess and tell him you quit."

"Why are you doing this to me?" Ariel asked, gripping her stone. "You know I need the job now. I need to take care of dad."

"I'm here to save your ass before you get burned," he said. "Look, I've got your back. Get inside the truck and — play along."

Ariel wanted to throw her stone, but she was stopped when a damp hand pressed into her shoulder. She flinched as it spun her around.

"Ariel, is this your father?" Pastor Meyer asked, masking his sarcasm with surprise.

"You know he's not my father," Ariel said to his unflinching grin.

Mr. Morales shook Pastor Meyer's hand with an unfounded gentleness. Ariel reveled at the double knowing look staring itself in the face. There was a slight jerk by Pastor Meyer, which was rebuked by Mr. Morales' turnover. The palm-on-palm lasted only a second before Pastor Meyer patted him on the back and glanced at Ariel's stone.

"Ariel was just telling me she wanted to tell you something important," Mr. Morales said.

"Of course. You know, we're here to support her," Pastor Meyer said.

"Yes, we all are."

Both men looked at her, expecting. What more could she do — but the eyes, the eyes were waiting. Closing in on her. Searching underneath her skin instead of her clothes. She looked for the pull, the instance she assumed control over their gaze with a swish of her hair or flick of a finger. Yet Mr. Morales and Pastor Meyer did not falter in their gazes.

"I'm quitting my job at Caballero. I'm sorry, pastor. I needed the money to pay for school."

After a beat, Pastor Meyer hugged her. He swayed, almost twisting her legs cemented in place. She thought she heard him muttering a prayer, but she expected nothing else. It was the fall of grace, it was the flight into home-born values, but Pastor Meyer had adopted the Latino sentimentality he had learned from BBQ fundraising rallies and dollar-store books. Pursing his lips, he straightened his shoulders and tilted his head downward. With his eyes still on Ariel's stone, he chuckled before replying with a smile.

"Ariel, you are forgiven. The lust of the flesh is a tempting thing. I will always be here if you need opportunities."

"My dad —"

"You are more than welcome to get your G.E.D. or apply to seminary schools up north. There's one in Wyoming that takes Faith students. Daniel's going up there this fall. You should ask him about it."

Blood dripped from Ariel's bitten tongue. As it trickled down her throat, she shivered with the taste of her life slipping away. It was all closing in too fast. She studied Pastor Meyer's demeanor, waiting for the moment to strike his blobbing body. But then Mr. Morales leaned forward and pinched her cheek. She shuddered faster than he could escape from the parking lot. She scrunched her eyes closed, but she could not erase the image of her personal Goliath limping away from her. His sandals flopped against dirt patches and crunched the fake grass until he reached his low-rider waiting on the curb. As his engine screamed, he waved his empty wallet out the window. Even Pastor Meyer appeared shocked, considering Ariel did not know whether his act was still on.

She had lost. She was done. But she needed to take something, anything back. She refused to end it all lacking the illusion of a choice. No more.

"I need a ride home," she said. It was true.

"That may not be —"

"Can you take me home?"

Unchanging in his expression, Pastor Meyer scratched the back of his hand. The instinctual grin pressed against his face, and then he sighed, satisfied with some unspoken thought. "Sure, give me about ten minutes."

Gently Ariel turned, but in her stride arose an unbridled energy noticed by lookers-on and the occasional passerby. It was her strut, her self-imposed limbo, that prolonged her waning moment of control. Sweat kissed her forehead and neck, burning tears froze in her eyes, but she was moving. Deliberate in her course, she made the school speak — termite-ridden wood crying out for a woman's touch, 1960s mini palm trees whistling catcalls — until she knew the place had recognized her place. Soon all the world was the courtyard as she slowed to a stop, staring into the passenger side of Pastor Meyer's truck. She saw dozens of hundred-dollar bills under the dashboard. Gray rubber band. Marked in black. Left in plain view — intentionally or lazily — and she could guess why. With Mr. Morales' words in mind, she held the handle, which loosened as she pulled. The door had been left unlocked.

Through the window, she saw Pastor Meyer's forehead glistening in the sunlight as he shifted from one side of the courtyard to the next, hand grasping and cheek kissing, constantly looking back at Ariel. The parents hugged and kissed him with a reverence otherwise saved for Christ statues. The men patted him on the back, resting their hands on his hunched shoulder-blades, while the women clasped his hands into theirs. They forgave his broken Spanglish. They accepted his Wisconsin otherness. They paid his price.

Minutes passed before the crowds thinned and Pastor Meyer could dart toward the truck. After she swung the door open, Ariel placed the bundle inside the glove compartment before he jumped inside, revved the engine, and pressed several radio and A/C buttons all in a rushed motion. He looked forward, then back, then toward the bottom of the seats, everywhere and anywhere except at Ariel.

"Corner of Kelly and Canaan," she said, pretending to ignore his distractedness.

Off onto Valley Road they went, a hidden tension following them. Pastor Meyer fidgeted in his seat, adjusting his height, rubbing the wheel. Ariel played keyboard on her thighs. Not even the shade underneath Expressway 83 and the infamous strip club itself, with the three-dog drifter sleeping under its "specials" sign, distracted her from the bundle that seemed to enlarge itself every second.

"You know, I've been meaning to meet your father. I lead an all-men's prayer group. Perhaps he can join when he's feeling better."

"He is part of it."

"Oh, well, I don't know about that," he said, lowering his head, not blinking.

"Both are part of it. Mr. Morales and my father."

"Who's Mr. Morales?"

A bump in the road, then Ariel reached for it. She clicked the compartment open and placed the bundle in the cup-holder. Pastor Meyer glanced at it, then at the road. They remained silent, waiting for another bump that never came. With less than two blocks left, he slowed down. His upper lip sucked on goatee remnants six days under-shaved. What few hints of joy leftover from sermonizing had faded into sagging neck-skin. At a stop sign, the truck's engine rumbled in a steady rhythm, its vibrations shivering down Ariel's spine. For the first time all day, she felt content.

"God bless you, Ariel. I thought I was doing the right thing, but God knew. He knew I was looking past your sin. And it took someone — one of my own men — to help me see. I don't see how Faith will survive. But I have hope. I hope you will redeem yourself. I did everything I could to support you. You don't have to thank me. Ariel, just get your documents and work honestly. For the Lord. He is our rock."

Ariel gripped her stone with trembling hands, the same hands that were once guarded by her father's holy intentions, but now were left to guide their own way after pleasuring poles and papis. Pastor Meyer extended his arm, but before he could touch her shoulder, Ariel opened the door and stepped onto the street. He called out her name, but the palm trees whooshing overhead sounded louder to her as she strutted away. The honking terrorized her until she threw the stone at the window, smiling at the miniscule crack before the truck sped on.

Embracing the heat rising from the streets, Ariel clasped her arms on her shoulders and walked through the darkening air, knowing uncertainty lurked down the road. From her porch, she could see the television screen cast shadows on the walls that jerked and twitched every two seconds in a frenzy of energy otherwise absent from the slumbering house. Inside, the flooring was cracked, the roof was molded, and the pipes were overheated — but patience was everywhere, hidden in the abyss of the house's age. The lingering smell of burnt tortillas guided her as she ghosted past the kitchen. She stood in front of her father sitting on the sanctuary couch, the right side of his face brightened by unsteady light, his mouth agape, eyes squinting. He chanted:

"God is good, God is good," he said. "Get to God, Ariel. Prosperers adhere."

He stood and hugged Ariel, their bodies forming one for a moment. Control relinquished. Touch numbed. All the while he nodded his head as if he knew something.

(2016)

WATCHER IN THE SKY

Chico knew nothing about the robotic aliens roaming his borderlands bubble. Had he read the newspapers, he would have known about nationwide surveillance regimes. If he could see into the future, he might have avoided ending his boyhood early by leaving alone the metallic creature fallen in the colonia's overgrown field. But there his summer discovery lay, nearly the size of two watermelons and about the same weight as his PlayStation 4. It looked otherworldly with its octopus-arms; miniature helicopter rudders attached to each. Now, church would have to wait.

Chico trekked through the green and golden weeds stained with the stench of taco wraps, lifting his legs above his hips, to inspect the alien. Not even the thought of Papa slapping his back, already bruised from freeze tag, could distract him from its dark hole eye. Blink, blink went the giant eyeball with its pink light. It mesmerized Chico, who only broke the trance by blinking in tune with the dying signal.

"I see you," Chico said, patting it. "I see me."

As he stared at his reflection, he thought the alien stuck out its tongue and contorted its face, not he. The longer he gazed at himself, the more his skin darkened into black. Then the bowl haircut disappeared. Buckteeth not noticed anymore. No more mouth and eyes, although he felt them widen in awe as he forgot where he stood. Eventually the reflection hardly existed anymore. He became the eyeball, simply watching. Like playing a new video game, the illusion continued for a lost time in the humidity of lazy midafternoon.

Then it was dark, and he could see Abuela picking underwear off the clothesline and Papa sitting on the porch lighting cigarettes and the van smoking with its hood open and he realized this was last night when he was asleep, yet he still saw it all in secret from above. He blinked and saw himself lying awake and uncovered and prostrate under the twirling fan and its shadows blanketing him in silence until he opened his eyes again.

He felt the sunrays closing in, burning the silence. The horizon seemed farther than before, and the field's sea of weeds shrunk as if deflated. Winds blowing warm reminders of reality, cars zooming south to Mexico, and mosquitoes sucking life from his skin all pulled Chico back. He shook his head, attempting to recreate the vision, but a rumbling sensation chilled his body until he twitched as if possessed. No Holy Spirit, just the eyeball continuing to blink, opening something inside of him he could not yet name. All he knew was that things looked differently — darker, even. His own hands appeared tinted with brown shades of something familiar. Brown grime, brown wrinkles, brown weight. The brown of Abuela and Papa. He could not name, but he could see.

"Vamos Chico! El tiempo se ha terminado."

Brown anger. Abuela's voice, having penetrated his playtime, rippled across his skin. He used to shrink from the shrill shriek, dashing back home along his adventure paths with his head drooped, dropping his swordsticks. But not today. As he fanned his sweat-clung-clothes, he resisted abandoning his newfound pet — toy? friend? alien? — and prayed for canceled church service. As he picked it up, Chico's arms weighed heavy with the alien's cold touch capped with the heat of a Sunday in Hidalgo and all its drowsy desires. He petted the eyeball, daydreaming of his alien's place in the family, but then realized he would have to ask Abuela first.

Across the street, Abuela leaned over the van's exposed engine, her body lanky with years of eighteen-wheeler journeys without air-conditioning. The van creaked with every wrench-twist as if mincing in pain at her strength, which Chico knew hid somewhere in her sagging skin. But her skin did not just sag anymore. Up the driveway, she looked younger against the wooden house, her brown skin glowing like never before. Despite the blood reddening her neck, her body looked stronger, as if she had grown younger. He thought he was seeing things, like when he imagined hawks circling overhead as she shared stories of her many river crossings. But now she looked like she had just risen from the river that morning. She was the groan of curanderas and the cucuy of nightmares, and now he would have to defend the alien from her wrath.

"¿Puedo quedármelo?" Chico asked, crossing the laneless road.

Abuela glared at the jet-black eyeball covering Chico's face and chest. Heat hovered between them, and so he stared back at Abuela. It had begun. Clenching his teeth, Chico, with chin upturned, ignored the scary power of the wrench in her hand. The longer Chico stared, the wider grew Abuela's smile like the ever-agreeable barrio abuela admired by children and winter Texans alike. But then she changed. He noticed her lips silently cursing the monster with verses memorized on missionary trips. The alien revved in response. A warm, silent buzzing that almost spoke. Then Abuela hissed at it. It was a slithering disapproval, seething and unknowing at the same time. But unlike the snakes Chico scavenged, Abuela wore her shed skin like armor. He still saw a lump of age standing before him, but not the Abuela he knew. Something beneath wanted to burst out.

After Abuela appeared frozen for a whole minute, Chico looked down and watched her in the glossy darkness. Her slump and absent gaze seemed like an illusion of the curved reflection, but when he glanced back at her, he knew she was gone. She knew too. She lost herself in an alternate telenovela universe, contemplating Mexico. Not old enough for the revolution, but not young enough for the men. The old world could never make her new, just stuck caring for chickens and trucks with no wings or wheels of her own. A jobless son graying her Latina locks. Too many days without shade.

Chico wanted to laugh at Abuela looking at the alien like it was a television. He tried, but it was too sad. Brown sadness. The same sadness he had ignored whenever he saw her struggle to bend down and pick up his toys, to write her signature on school papers, to spank the dashboard until the engine started. And there she was, baking in the skin she was born in. He had expected her to look away, but he was forced to place both hands on the eyeball to pull her back.

"Pregúntale a tu padre," she said in a deep voice.

A sugar-rush adrenaline filled Chico, who placed the alien on the chicken-littered yard and hopped through the rickety door to the kitchen, relieved. He passed chairs on top of the table, mops blocking the fridge, family-set of Bibles on the counter; it was mass time.

"I found something. It's on the lawn," Chico said, half-hoping his voice would not find Papa.

"¿Qué es?"

"Un extraterrestre."

After a minute of flies buzzing around the restroom knob, the word seemed to sneak under the door, ending Papa's pre-church ritual. His gut jiggled, soft and sweaty, powerless and puffy. Floppy brown. It made Chico sad knowing that he could have stopped Papa from eating so many candy bars if he had just realized it sooner. Papa was no longer Papa the Boxer, or El Chapo.

"Papa, you're fat. I'm gonna help you get strong again."

"Cállate, cabron."

Magazine in hand, Papa limped toward the open window. His bad foot dragged across the tile-broken floor, and Chico flinched at its colors. Brown and black and blue. Chico's feet were strong enough to climb twenty-foot trees, yet he still connected himself to Papa's foot. He remembered watching the foot glide across boxing rings, tickle him as he wiggled on the floor. With the foot came food and toys, which had slowly stopped after Papa stayed home more often. He and the foot were tied up like shoelaces, one looping past the other until now.

Papa stared at the alien. Chico could not see what he saw, but he stood still, taking it in.

"Es un helicóptero. No alien. Basura," he said.

"No, no!"

Then began the stamping tantrum Chico had mastered in kindergarten. In Mexico, the teachers thought it was a devil deep inside, but Papa had met the devil while crossing the Rio Grande and knew nonsense when he saw it. Also, the teachers had never tried slapping Chico on the back. So, he did. Chico coughed in exaggerated pain until he inched closer to the foot and kicked it. He did not know why, but it made him feel better.

Papa cried. He slid a chair off the kitchen table and leaned against it, lifting his foot to wipe away the blood. Chico had never seen

Papa bleed. Not even men twice his size could stain Papa's brown skin with red. He felt strong yet puzzled. It was Papa. He was the strongest of them all, yet Chico had made him bleed.

Abuela glared at Chico through the window, her soft voice contradicting her eyes' menace.

"No lo golpees," she said, but she did not look at either of them.

She grasped the windowsill with a scowl confusing to Chico, who now saw the creases in her face again, as if she had just grown up. Then there was the frightened Papa, who did not know what to do with his trembling fist. But it was the one-second-look between Papa and Abuela that confused his boy mind. No authority, just pursed lips. No control, either, just raised eyebrows. As close as they were physically, Chico felt farther from them than before. Their eyes peeked past him, invisible, as if he weren't in the house anymore. He yearned for the eyeball so he could see what made them so angry.

"Papa, what did you see when you looked at the alien?" Chico asked.

"Nada. No es E.T," Papa said straightening his back, caught off guard.

Chico looked to Abuela for help, but she simply nodded her head.

"E.T. makes me see things," he said, unable to articulate what he did not understand. "Let it stay!"

"Pobrecito, he needs glasses. Hey, maybe I pawn it for glasses tomorrow," Papa said.

With that, the chickens stopped squabbling. And with the silent tension, there came that familiar family forgetting spell: erasing unpleasant memories to maintain the illusion of togetherness in a lonely corner of the country. Abuela knew it from years of dinnertime hugs following fieldwork fights, and Papa felt the burden of her wasted church tithes and her bedside kisses. But all Chico could think about was E.T. waiting for its playmate, and the itch behind his right knee. Despite their strange gazes, he ran around Papa's legs and, escaping Abuela's grasp, hauled E.T. across the street and back into the fields.

As Chico staggered in the high grass, the blinking light emitting from E.T. began to dim, and when he completed the trek, he felt farther from home than ever. But the specter of Abuela and Papa's eyes urged him to stay hidden, alone with the only other being who could see what he saw. So went the waiting game busy with scratchy knees nearly bloody from tripping over E.T. Cheeks red from the sun, Chico sat facing away from his house, poking E.T.'s eyeball.

Then he escaped. He found himself flying alongside E.T. and gliding past hundreds and hundreds of heads and hats and dogs below and blue sky and clouds and birds above. Bounding, tumbling, fleeing, zipping past the house and church and school and fields and everywhere that taught him how to think before everything faded into his childhood memories. But now he saw all the colors of fear and adulthood and workaday afternoons pouring down like rain on faces unknown but familiar, unseen yet tracked, stained with the uncertainty of tomorrow.

One vision showed the family outside of church, and Chico spotted himself with the blue tie and the ripped pants and the shoes so big they slipped with every step. He followed the van as it drove home with Abuela at the wheel waving Papa's cigarette smoke out the window. The front right tire was losing air and the engine roared too loudly as he slept in the backseat waiting for after-church fast food. He never wondered how he saw it all, but he did wonder who else could see it all.

It was a treat, a vomit roller coaster, a dizzy insanity, but soon it all turned dark. He found himself inside of the eyeball. No longer looking outward, but inward at the blinking light. He reached for it, but he could not see his hands or legs. It was like falling into the abyss, floating in darkness, chasing shadows.

Then the light died. Nothing left to see.

Eventually two suns appeared, black in the burn. A white face filled in behind them. Chico shielded himself from the sunglass eyes. When he peered past his fingers, he realized he was in his own living room. He witnessed the woman in green uniform sitting in the armchair across from Abuela, who was sunken into the loveseat with a tight smile on her face. He felt confused until Abuela's grasp finally caught him and pulled him close to her lap. Still dizzy from the flight, Chico heard only snippets from the sunglass woman's mouth.

"Drone program...illegals..."

"What did you do to him?" Chico asked, pointing at E.T. upside-down on the floor.

The sunglass woman towered over Chico. When she kneeled to face him, he noticed how her rotten-milk skin clashed with his own as if it were a white crayon scratching out the brown underneath. Smooth like his own, but different. A difference that made him afraid to look into her eyes, which were not unlike E.T.'s eyeball.

"He's resting right now. Long night looking for aliens."

"But he's E.T. He is an alien."

"I saw you playing alien with him."

"I was flying."

"Yes, you were heavy. Why didn't you leave E.T. where you found him?"

"He's mine. He made me an alien too."

Abuela covered his mouth, her touch chilling him.

"No es un alienígena," Abuela said, her voice cracking.

With clenched fists, Chico beat against the sofa until Abuela seized his arms. He growled, glancing back at the sunglass woman to fix the problem.

"Perdón," Abuela said. "Chico no sabes —"

The sunglass woman lifted her hand, silencing Abuela. Chico awed. What power, what magic. It made Abuela sit back. It made Abuela like him: small and quiet, waiting for the next word.

"Why did you say you're an alien?" the sunglass woman asked.

"Because I've seen things through E.T."

"Like what?"

"Different stuff. E.T. showed me lots of people. I also saw Abuela's face, Papa's belly."

Leaning her head to the side, the sunglass woman smirked. Chico attempted to see her eyes, but he only saw his enlarged head. No visions, just himself and Abuela sitting behind him with her hands on her lap. In this reflection, she seemed calm, accepting. Waiting for something like sleep or church to happen like it always had. But also, sad. Sadder than earlier. It made Chico sad.

"Do you know any other aliens?"

"No, just E.T."

The sunglass woman glanced at Abuela, then back at Chico.

"No others?"

Chico searched for the answer in Abuela's eyes, which softened into tired puddles of years. Her silent, moving mouth seemed to speak more curses learned over a lifetime of hiding in plain sight.

"No, Abuela doesn't even believe E.T. is an alien."

As she stood, the sunglass woman surveyed the living room once more.

"Well, it's time for E.T. to go home."

"No!"

Without any more words, the sunglass woman picked up E.T. and left the house. She revved the white truck parked outside and sped away, dirt trails following. Chico teared up.

"Pinche migra," Papa said, emerging from the restroom. Hands on hips, he peered out the window with his tongue out. Then Abuela stood and slapped his back.

"Cobarde."

"Eh? No soy estúpido, vieja bruja."

With E.T. gone, Chico felt like disappearing. He listened to Abuela and Papa argue for the first time, their faces grim like the pastors at confession.

"No entendí nada de lo que dijo," she said.

"Blah blah, she deports you later."

"¿Qué? Primero te deportaré."

She slapped Papa's face. Chico flinched, afraid of what might happen if he were to sneak past their legs and run toward the fields.

"Stop fighting," Chico said. "Or I'll go with E.T. too!"

"Yes, you an alien," Papa said, laughing loudly. "Me too. She too."

Papa's laugh reverberated off the walls and into the street. The chickens outside fluttered, and Abuela objected with a raised hand. But the hand did not stop Papa. He continued laughing, almost doubling over. When Papa became tired, Chico watched him slouch into the loveseat, his face blank.

The silent tension returned along with the family forgetting spell. A long pause, and then the heat-ray day continued.

"Then we're all aliens," Chico said. "We're real. I told you."

He stomped onto the tile, cracking its corner. It sounded as if the house were in pain.

"Ay, Chico. Vamos a prenderle una vela a E.T," Abuela said.

Now she laughed, snickering softly at first, then with wheezes and gasps as Papa accompanied her with a light stream of chuckles along with his imitation of E.T.'s long arms.

"Si, si. We late for mass," he said.

Hopping up and down, Chico squealed in approval.

"We might see E.T. there."

(2017)

LA LOMITA

Dana, oh Dana, my dear depressive. It was that time of the week when my sister's skin would turn ghost white and through the walls she went toward La Lomita Chapel. Every chapel run meant another trip to the confession box, escaping the mad angels fluttering through her brain and scavenging the Rio Grande riverbank for her reflection, but I knew there was more to it. She would return home calm and smiling at 2 AM as if it were all some Whataburger run, and now her stomach was showing it. Forget genetics; this was lovelorn-Catholicism-church-going guilt gone bad. As I stood in the doorway watching her sofa rhapsody full of tears, I decided I would beat her there to see for myself whether I should move out or invest in more pills.

Like Mother long before me, I barreled west toward Dana's Mecca. We used to have another family there. The guilty sinners were our cousins, the towering Jesus Christ statue was the father we never had, and the border patrol agents were our cranky uncles. When I was a kid, they kept me company while Dana wailed to god and kissed the Virgin Mary. Every trip was like coming home until her mind stopped us — sisters with the same ashy forehead — from returning. Now deeming me "loveless and unworthy," Dana ventures back every week alone in her disillusionment, hoping for someone to save her in that ancient building, just a woman of sorrows trapped in a never-ending routine.

Turning into the gravel road, I stared at the cross high in the darkening sky, wondering if Dana had somehow beaten me here. After I parked, the heat boiling from the bushlands slowed my approach to the chapel. The sun touched the top of the eastward hill separating me from civilization, and to the west the Rio Grande flowed with an uneasy placidity; another world lay two hundred meters that way. Why Dana never crossed I could not say, although I assumed she tried since she sometimes returned with wet shoes.

Alone, I slid my hand against the white paint seeping off the brick, absorbing the dust that had clung to this relic of borderland sanctity. The candlelight at the far end of the chapel burned dimly; the dark swallowed the smoke. Even in the fading light, I could read the broken English prayers written on dollar-store notebooks strewn across the ground. Maybe mine was in there somewhere — twelve years old, a future ex-social worker whose sister would be her unsolved case.

I sat in the back pew, flat on my ass with no Dana. With a sigh, I checked my phone for the dozen messages she had sent telling me to hurry back, she needed me nearby, the world was dead. I closed my eyes and entered the in-between world of dreams and reality where everything and nothing was dead; there in the blurriness, all twenty-seven of my years separated from me and transformed into blazing flashes of memory about the Rio Grande Valley where the sun set on two different worlds that bled onto one another, their people crossing and dying every day, and I wished I wouldn't have been born ten miles away from the river where Dana would probably drown herself.

Helicopter roars. I looked out the prison-gated window obscuring the moonlight. Only black. Turning on my phone's flashlight, I stood but stumbled over a misplaced brick. The helicopter's engine grew louder, and in my panic, I flashed my light over the Christ figurines with sad and concerned eyes looking this way and that, across the chapel and down at the uneven bricks, concealing secrets and mysteries. Jesus was staring at everything but me.

The noise from above died down, replaced by breathing. Then I heard footsteps coming closer. A hand touched my shoulder. The figure shined a light on me, and I pointed my phone toward it, our ghost-lights crisscrossing over one another in an ecstasy of confusion, until a glare reflected off the "Border Patrol" badge on his chest. Urgency flared across his face, oddly silent.

"¿Dana? Dana mi querida?"

The voice sounded from behind the altar. Desperate for calm, I held my breath as the agent approached it. And then the shadow on the wall exploded. Dark and brown-eyed, dripping wet and shivering, holding up two bloodied hands that shielded his face from the light but exposed the ribs protruding from his body, he revealed a lonely terror that strikes those who would rather die than be seen; he grasped his head, and his eyes betrayed the fear that erupted from his soul, spewed forth from his toothless mouth.

"¡No estoy listo para casarme, Dana!"

He bulleted past me and out of the chapel and up the levee and onto that South Texas road rolling beyond our sight. The agent followed. Stuck between end-of-the-world sadness at the tip of Texas and the edge of madness at the borders of Mexico, I too embraced the thought of escape. And in my thrall, I remembered Dana, lying prostrate on our sofa, staring at the mold-encrusted ceiling, waiting for death while here I stood face-to-face with death, not wishing it on anyone.

Shaking, I stepped out into the sweltering night, where the Border Patrol truck and two police cars glowed under the moon. Dana sat in the backseat behind a policeman. She smiled, sinister and solemn in her vengeance on who knows what, rubbing her belly. Passing and passing, the cars over the hill went their own way in the common dark of all our destinations.

(2016)

THE CURANDERA ON
ALAMEDA STREET

The housewives are on TV, and I feel alive. Volume's on low so I can look instead of listen and watch the dead pixels prove the pawn shop right. Fifty-four-thirteen they said, which is only eleven or twelve meals gone. Mom got a lot on layaway after my legs started acting like stubs and lounging became my afterschool pastime. Only thing I can do with my belly bulging out. Up in Jersey those housewives don't look like this, or the cameras don't show it at least. But no need to think about it until it happens, no.

"No naming until it happens," Mom said to me when we found out. "Don't even think about it. God will punish you for every thought."

Now Mom's at the kitchen counter cutting tomatoes to the rhythm of some cumbia and I don't even understand the words. Swinging those hips hardened by middle-age and all those days bending over unmade hotel beds, munching on gum because the day goes and goes and goes, no time for facial cream, much less dinner, and flipping that knife with a twist of her fingers numb from the arthritis painkillers. It's as if she never had me and made it in New York. She likes doing this, putting herself in that bubble I can't pop. My bubble belly doesn't help either. Every day she gives me el ojo as if I'm still fourteen. She learned that look of shame from the Catholic women's group, and it's like she can see right through me and feel the kicks and smell the diapers already and — don't even think about it.

"Dios me perdone por mis pecados. We can't afford it," she said while staring at me. "We can say something happened. People will feel bad."

After her insulin shot, Mom jangles her car keys in front of me, and I know it's time. I can't complain. Any day Mom gets me out of school is a good day, although it'll probably involve a foot rub tonight. She hands me the plastic bag full of tomato slices while she pats herself down in front of the living room mirror, straightening her dress a size too tiny. I open the door and the humidity hugs me, reminding me that I'm in South Texas and not South Jersey. A housewife series in the making, and Mom doesn't even care.

"Anyone?" Mom asks, and I twist around to check but I see all the stuff in the back — student athlete Bibles, women's clinic brochures, toilet paper — and imagine what Dad would say if he wasn't working en otro lado because I know he loves order when he can get it.

I shake my head and soon wish I had said something because the rest of the ride is quiet, except for the speed bumps everywhere on Eldora Road. As if Mom hits them on purpose. No wonder we seem taller than those weeds, where who knows what's growing since the Valley is all humid heat and flatness and sometimes there's just flat heat. I feel bad for those group of boys running in a pack on the shoulder like a dignified bunch. They're a football field away and they look like they're running away from us, so I assume Isaac must be with them since he's been running away from me since he found out. Or maybe they must know about Mom's random rages and why she shouldn't drive anything weighing more than a ton. The farther away you are from Mom's car, the farther away you can move. Whenever I would bring up college, Mom would say you just want the white men, you can't be trusted up-state. Funny to think Isaac and I live blocks away.

Soon the boys pass away, and the San Juan Basilica comes into view, the giant Jesus and Mary welcoming us as we exit the expressway. Why does the Virgin close her eyes? I remember asking Mom when I was younger. Because she was painted that way! And then I blurt the words "that way" because Mom's turning every direction, not knowing which way to go. I didn't know which way either, but some way was better than no way. I remember saying something like that after my missed my period and — it's 3rd period right now with Mrs. Cruz and I know the class is pretending to read — bye-bye, brown Jesus, as we turn the corner and circle around the Basilica, Mom swishing her silent cross signs.

Alameda Street is somewhere, but I don't look for it, since I know that a street can be judged by its smell. No palm tree gulf breeze here, just sewer. We almost pass it by until Mom makes a hard stop and turns into the car-filled-street with houses that all look the same. What house would dare look different in front of that Basilica? Better to look all good than some bad and others better when Jesus is looking and Mary's floating over the Rio Grande. The frontage road is cut off from the neighborhood by uncut grass, apparently Jesus is hiding us from any drive-by church ladies, and I stare at the cars zooming by until we slow down, meaning Mom's found the place: a slanted house with a grey roof, but I don't see nothing special about it.

"Smile, Rita," Mom says as we walk up the curb, believing we're being watched like on some reality TV show and there's no retakes.

Knocking twice, and with me standing behind her, Mom waits until a fat mustached man answers and then takes my hand in hers. Like those happy families on the news blessed by a random turkey donation at Christmastime. She pushes me forward and the man knows. He opens the door wider, letting Mom pull me past the dingy living room full of cats and DVDs and unwashed kitchen plates and smelling like Febreze mixed with weed. I'm still carrying the plastic bag, which gives me weird looks from the boys lying on the couch staring at who knows what before we walked in. Mom snatches it from me after we pass into the backyard, and the light I had just seen in front seems brighter here in this patch of weeds mowed ten months ago. Only a beaten-up shed, slanting on one side, stands there like a giant doghouse.

"This woman is going to show you the way to becoming a better woman," Mom says after the man shuts the door and closes the blinds.

She repeats the line again when we get to the shed, except this time we wait at least a whole minute until the door creaks open. At least my chewed-up fingers don't look like that veiny, nail-less hand emerging from the darkness, snatching a tomato slice, and throwing it inside a thin mouth. I could hear the chewing, though, which let me know that this person at least ate like us. The door opens, and I see that it's a wrinkled woman, too old, I figure. A rag is wrapped around her head, probably bald, and she stares at me and gives me el ojo. A different kind from Mom's, as if she's angry not at me, but for me. Scowling, I give her my own look, silently judging her loose Goodwill clothing and apron-like gown.

She turns back inside without even a hello, and we follow her.

Herbs in the corner, hand drums in the other, baskets dangling from the ceiling, little figurines that I saw sold at yard sales, beads hanging from rusted nails, and there isn't even a toilet. The shed's wood is wet and moldy after all the rain from the past thousand years and the sweat that keeps falling off this old lady, who looks like she'll die any minute. She stands behind a table and Mom and I sit on the floor. I couldn't sit cross-legged if a camera crew paid me.

The old lady is still chewing that same tomato slice. Noisy, no, but irritating, and I wish there was a fly or something else to make some other sound that would distract me from staring at Mom in thirty years. I glance at her, and she seems even more confused than me.

"Ma'am," Mom says. "For almost six months, my daughter —"

"Ay, embarazada," the old lady says with a nearly toothless grin.

They both chuckle, but I know what that word means. It's the same word Isaac said over the phone when I told him. Always fancy with words and carrying around books with titles like Saving Capitalism and wanting to be proven right, so I even looked embarazada up on the internet and double checked in the dictionary just to say, "You're right, baby."

Ah, baby — it's like I'm flying past fields and rivers and people going about their day, smoking on corners and drinking coffee on the go. I blink and the images go away, but when I open my eyes again there's the influencer on, I saw YouTube talking about the different kinds of baby formula, baby shoes, baby toys, baby everything. Like an old camera, I'm shutting and opening my eyes to memories I thought I had forgotten — must be the smell in here.

"¿Y el padre?" I hear the old lady ask Mom.

I know those words too, and Isaac's naked body is in front of me now, grinning and eyeing my thighs. Slick boy, I remember how he played me the first time, saying something about numbers and I listened like I had a degree in Math. The school bell had rung but we rushed into the locker room and did it before the boys changed for P.E. No, Mom, I did not have sex, the cameras were wrong. No, Isaac, I'm not interested anymore. But both were lies and I ended up on my back more than once just like now, lying on the old lady's table, staring at the lightbulb.

"She's performing a limpia," Mom says as the old lady cleans my tummy with egg juice and rosemary.

Might as well have someone come in and start banging on the drums, then at least it'd be entertaining like that night on Dad's ranch. Back then I was a country girl. Moonshine made me clear-minded, and the music never stopped until I said so. Go, go go! The guitarist would rub his fingers all over the strings, his cowboy hat covering his face, and the drummer would BAM! a cymbal every five seconds. Isaac knew the beat, and he knew I knew the beat too. And then we were gone, the drum tapping to our stomps on the hay. Weslaco never knew a louder party than my quince. Even now that it's over, the purity ring Dad gave me before he and Mom had that argument over bills, and he left with a suitcase saying adios still shines like it's brand new. He said not to take it off until he comes back, so it goes in the shower too.

"Ándale! Sin no more!"

The old lady continues chanting the words, her Spanglish fluttering out of the shed like a shrieking chihuahua. Rougher, rougher on my belly with every chant, and soon it hurt every time she switched languages. In the corner of my eye, Mom stands with her usual angry-looking face staring at me being straightened out like a meat patty. The stench from the egg is like an exorcism taking place on my skin and I feel like leaving my body and standing beside Mom and poking inside her spirit for once. Maybe it's murkier than mine, but at least I can have my revenge. I want to think that I can see my body on the table as my spirit sits on the drums, but I know I'm too attached to myself for that. I stay with myself, like a good girl, not like when Isaac stopped texting me twice a day and blocked me from Instagram and just disappeared once the second trimester came by. All the good men leave to do something even greater, like the Marines or some other military thing, Dad used to say. I could find another man, but not while looking like a Latina balloon. Worry about it when it happens.

Although I know I'm in a shed, all that egg makes hazy and crazy pictures pop up. Mom cradling it like she always wanted it, which makes sense because she didn't push it out but also doesn't make sense because of the budget. Dad locking away his suitcase and building a crib in the storage room and sleeping in the bedroom from now on so I can use the sofa. The shirtless boys running into my arms and my legs shake because there's Isaac in the front, short shorts and sweating, grabbing my hair and making me beg. And then there's the belly swelling to the size of a watermelon and reality with a gloved hand starting to hit me harder than Mom ever did. It could happen.

In the pain and in the moment, I thought a thought I sometimes thought but never thought I could think so clearly as I did now: I was being made into a female Frankenstein and Mom never asked me for my opinion. The minute she found out she was calling clinics all over Texas, asking about costs and wait lists and procedures that were too complicated for her to understand. A drive-by usually meant watching a parade of men in baseball caps wave colorful cardboard signs and block the entrance. Such a fancy way of saying no.

Well, like Dad used to say: If you can't be right, be quiet. One weekend, it's all rainbows and baby bibs with Mom, when she would even stop bringing her signs to those clinic meet-ups. Then Monday rolls around and she's looking at my baby photos and my belly like they're before-and-after pictures of a hurricane. And she'll never forget the day I got out of the car and got pointed at by the old abuela next door, or at least she'll never make me forget it. It left her so tired that night she just nodded as if knowing something when one of my friends came over and said something about a pill.

Then Mom turned to the men in red ties on TV, who still couldn't convince her otherwise even though they yelled numbers and figures and big words during debates. Im-mo-ra-li-ty! In-fi-del-i-ty! But Mom just switched the channel to golf and let the clapping put her to sleep. Not even our pastor gave her the weekly blessing after listening to her confession. Just verses and curses, verses and curses.

I knew about it when our pulpit pals avoided eye contact with me, but then began eyeing Mom with a strange look somewhere in between cuddling a dead kitten and smelling rotten milk.

"So, what's the answer?" Mom asks, bringing me back. "To get rid of it?"

The question sounded like a cliffhanger that would always give me time to get a snack or stretch my legs, but the old lady had no time for commercials.

"¿Que? No!" the old lady says. "Ella esta demasiado gorda ahora. Too fat."

It's happening. And like that, everything transforms into a telenovela with Mom exploding into a hurricane of insults in English and Spanish and some other language while the old lady stands silently chewing on the tomato slices, maybe her only lunch and dinner for the next three days until she rose from the dead and asked for cabbage. To my ears, it sounds like no more church meetings and fancy Bible dinners.

"I don't want her to go through what I went through," Mom said in that voice she usually saves for church.

"She's gone, mamá! Ándale. Sin no more!" the old lady says again, waving us away.

Mom pulls my tumbling body past the yard, banging on the screen door with a fury usually seen on season finales, and through the house and into the car all in one of those larger-than-life moments that take up time but happen in no time. Now we're really speeding over those bumps. Hope Jesus doesn't see us, or else a state trooper stuck in afternoon traffic will stop Mom during one of her moods and we'd go to jail for sure. All that brush along the road can't cover up a crime, all that sin can't hide in tires like the drug dealers at checkpoints, all that stuff Mom puts into her Sunday barbacoa can't make me sleepy enough to forget it almost didn't happen. So, I finally give myself permission to decide Matthew if it's a boy, Alexandria if a girl.

"What does Dad think?" I ask before Mom pulls into our driveway.

"Dad doesn't need to know."

Mom parks and heads inside, although her screams leave the house before the door shuts. I follow, feeling the grass rise against my stumpy ankles, wondering if Isaac has texted back. Inside, I lie down on the couch, too lazy to wash the egg off. It is kicking. I had forgotten to turn off the TV, and I remember the housewives marathon goes on until eight. But Mom is rustling through Dad's suits and ripping them off the hangers. She clicks her nails against the metal, like a personal tune. Head low, she returns to her usual spot behind the kitchen counter and tears up before hanging everything up again. When she emerges from the hallway with a pocket Bible, I think about asking her about it, but figure not to bother a woman in pain. Besides, the commercials are over.

(2016)

BURN THE SUN

It's sunrise, and Sabas pounds his chest as he strides across the SpaceX parking lot. No matter how fast he moves, he feels the heat closing in — sun rays, lingering rocket fumes, Gulf Stream air, and the boss man following close behind. In the boss man's hands Sabas' resignation, and in Sabas' hands his chest heavy with years. He feels the brown skin burning beneath, as well as the rumble of a 1993 Thunderbird.

"You can't just quit, Sabas," says the boss man, yelling through the engine's scream. "Blame the suits for the Mars bullshit, not me!"

Yawning, Sabas shields himself from the sun, pretending to snatch it in his hand as if expecting a catch, but no fish swim in that stardust stream. Absurdity of number flows through that astral vision: space coasts and galaxy ports align the vacuums up there, unbound, no place for infinitesimal rockets — but plenty for human spirits, he notes. The beeping of his watch glaring in the sunlight is in tune with the universe and Carlita's engine, marking the beginning of the suicide plot.

"Cabron! Don't make me call Homeland!" says the boss man.

The door to the Thunderbird jerks open and in Sabas goes, flipping off the boss man and licking the sweat off his upper lip. Against the wind the Thunderbird flies, roaring louder than the gulf coast waves, revving toward the road jetting westward until it all hits — the cracked speed booms against the boss man's yells, and the heat of blood rises in Sabas as he gropes Carlita's shoulder. In his mind he dominates her body born brown without the need for papeles, his fever dream. But she leans over the wheel, in her eyes the future: All the miles on the road leading toward another couch while Sabas disappears in the rearview mirror — a vision she would make real soon, she reassures herself.

"I told him I knew he was shutting down the project for weeks. He doesn't know about the shack," Sabas says, eyeing the rearview mirror and the smartphone in the boss man's hands snapping the getaway.

"The boy swears he did it with yagé, so I got an appointment with Dr. De La Cruz at noon," Carlita says in a yell too quiet for Sabas' old ears but too loud to maintain her too-cool-to-care composure.

Ripping off the DRAGON PROPULSION ENGINEER work-tag and loosening his tie, Sabas stares at Boca Chica Boulevard zooming past in a bored blur, fitting for the Rio Grande Valley's forgotten corner where there are no saints nor scientists, only madmen crushed by the weight of the country. Twenty miles straight on that street and the potholes of Brownsville's colonias would soon flame his sight, but his imagination rests beyond the Texas cloud-ridden sky, through light-years, onto Mars — as Carlita twirls her black curls, sighing. Astral projection, he told her every day, was the key to that planet of failed funding. Today, he assumes she knows.

Emerging from the Thunderbird, Sabas hears the muffled moans escape from the shack damp from last night's rainfall, the deluge having showered through holes in the roof. Carlita inspects the walls before unlocking the six latches and witnessing their experiments. Inside the shack, people are littered throughout. Carlita's tired face absorbs the shadows exploding from her lighter. She drags her cig, inhaling deep as she walks up to Jose's burnt body prostrate in the center, searching for a pulse. Dead, Sabas knows, and had he withstood the flame tests the final interviews would have been revelatory. But he knew Jose had seen visions while on the edge, living yet covered in the light of his ethereal spirit, free from the constraints of the flesh and inching toward that unreachable red Mecca unknown to the SpaceX suits and wrench-twisters.

"Mars is lonesome for her star-rover!" Sabas says, circling the room and eyeing Carlita's yagé brews in the far corner.

The moans from that unnamed teen who skateboarded through the Porter Zoo on weekends intensify until, annoyed, Sabas sits beside the muzzled and handcuffed boy.

"She said you did it three days ago," Sabas says while removing the mask. "Tell me what you saw."

Bloody spit spatters on Sabas' face, and he mounts the boy and grasps his pimpled face, carving his fingers into the nostrils until the shaking and shivering stops.

"You at home calm-faced reading hypnosis books at desk," the boy says. "Frida Kahlo portrait next to the door in bedroom, three green pills by the lamp, girl waiting for you outside in green Thunderbird."

"Ah, shut up," he says laughing. "You were in my casa! You saw my red briefs! Why'd you come back here?"

"I could've stayed gone. It's like a little death man, no heaviness. Like there's no gravity. But there's no fixes out there without a body, so what's the use of flying without the feeling, you know…"

Lifting the container by his side and drawing the needle and hitting the vein in the crook of the arm, Sabas sates the boy, quiet now and watching with an uncaring glare at Carlita sitting on the other side of the shack. Silence — until Carlita rolls her eyes and coughs forcefully. Sabas throws a wad of cash at her feet. She lunges for it, counts each bill.

"Last payment unless the experiment fails. You stay until it works," he says.

"Honestly, shoulda given it another month. Margin of error or something. What if he's lying? Injecting yagé can do some brain damaging shit."

Sweat beads fall, and on the unevenly-planked floor Sabas stares into an abyss, repressing his fears, calming the calamities in his mind — the cops, FBI, Homeland Security, the heat closing in. All before the burn that would separate himself from his body and prove he is the spirit inside, and the spirit never dies. As engineer and Mexican, he proved wrong the naysayers laughing at his "pachuco pout-face" and the curanderos prophesying that his brownness was his bane. As star-rover and spirit, he would reach Mars, the epitome of his pain. Into the abyss he stretches his hand, grasping at blackness darker than his brown skin, and clenches his fist hoping to transform himself into any other color.

"The Feds would've found me out next month during regulatory review," he says. "With the Mars mission called off, what else do I do but try out the research now?"

"Shoulda pretended to be Sabas 'Nix' insteada 'Mosqueda.' Now they're giving your spot to a gringo."

The word burns bitter but true. He imagines childhood reveries of flying higher, like the airplane that roared over his stepmom's house on long Sunday afternoons before church. At its zenith, the plane shadowed the sun and Sabas would grasp it in his hand. Clutching and unclutching his fist in triumph, he would become the airplane, flying free. As if the shadow sucked the brown from his body, he felt no burn, only power. He would surge across the yard and onto the street and through the neighbor's bushes, unaware of the invisible border between his space and that space. His body ignored space as he cut across lawns and cut in line at the international bridge and cut between his father and mother's fights — until the day his father cut his chest.

Now the dominant hand which had beat his father pounds his scarred chest, always hidden by the white-collared shirt. It never stings, only burns in the heat. With newfound vigor, he breathes the musty stench of death and piss and burnt flesh and proclaims, "Gringos have never been to Mars!"

Carlita rolls her eyes. Their red-brown abysses reflect imagined murder-scenes and castrations, silently fulfilling Sabas' death wish. What else could she do but project her visions through her eyes, dilations, and all? Sabas could see them: If she could take one moment into her hands, she would stop the wheel of torpor that kept her moving, moving from one madman to the next. That false vitality that attracted her to Sabas was the dead end she always feared, like an uncrossable border. He sees himself in her pupils forlorn. He attempts to look away, but he gleams in that galaxy within her gaze, gasping for air. He hears his final swallow. He feels his throat tighten. He readies his fist, but his stare is broken by a car alarm.

The siren jolts Sabas and Carlita toward the Thunderbird as a flock of birds flies past Boca Chica Boulevard, soon silent again.

They look at one another again, but without seeing. In those heartbeat seconds, they were only two border-crossers with the shared desire to rid themselves of a body. Sabas' watch beeps 10:30 AM, needle time. He rushes toward the container and positions himself beside the boy. Surrounded by an aura of smoke, Carlita leans against the entrance and observes the desperate scene.

"Dr. De La Cruz will push you over if the yagé doesn't," she says in a mocking tone.

Calming his heavy breathing, Sabas remembers the Golden Dawn vatos and Chinese compadres who practiced their power through projection. The needle drips. He envisions the boss man sitting in the office flipping away at his files. The needle punctures. He mouths the words "Reynosa-born and Matamoros-raised" and "graduate of Tecnológico de Monterrey" — which could never explain the bum burning the side-streets of his brain every day. The needle injects. He imagines sitting in the engine room surrounded by bureaucratic monsters munching away at his medicine. Clear-minded and mystical without it, he knows. The needle drops. He sees equations float onto the walls before they all fall away, revealing dead ocelots under the ground and lightyear possibilities above the sky, eroding his body-border.

Dosage higher, ingredients varied, bloodstream frenzied. Reality sizzles into heat and boredom. Intensity of vision and lucidity of thought — ants heaving a pebble beside Jose's open eyes have found a pedestal for their aristocracy — marks the tenth minute but time rushes counterclockwise. Into the passenger seat, the body that's forgotten its name sits on polyester melting the nostrils and inhales smoke staining the taste buds while Carlita rubs the shoulder with hands that know few wiped tears.

"Act cool," she says.

Checkpoint, checkpoint, checkpoint of uniforms and interviews lines the street with cars waiting for the split. Exhaust fumes fuel the brain with la migra memories with their green-line trucks parked outside the stonewall building where the visa slept unconfirmed until the mighty machine swallowed its dynamos and granted another induction token. Believing in the needle's lies, the scene morphs into a judgment of the self. Now Carlita sits in that office, at least two years before the first hook-up after B.Y.O.B. night at the dry cantina, shaking her head full of fourth-generation Mexican American skepticism. Fragmented and bordered, her eyes speak.

"Are you a U.S. citizen?" he hears.

A nod and two passports, then giggles. The glee of homecoming. She jerks a lever to roll up the window, but it transforms the car into a doctor's office instead. A doctor looking like Carlita injects an unexplainable paranoia of white suits into Sabas, who sinks into his seat. Sad-faced and bug-eyed, she signs prescriptions under the order of the subconscious, eager to please the primal urge to suffocate patients with pillowcases. Dysmorphia, dysmorphia, she writes on a notepad, beginning her first poem.

"To the phantoms that slip into the crevices of the skull," she says, as if reading from an off-screen teleprompter. "The truth of craziness is sanity's lie and nobody and no body is safe. Including you, asshole."

Falling off the peak, Sabas reminds himself of his body. It hits — the car rides, the drugs and alcohol and goofy sex, the insecurities — junk sickness forces his legs to curl up. He retches until the passenger door opens and he chokes out his plea.

"Get rid of this body."

"We will. We're here."

Sabas leans back, feeling swallowed by windows, passive in his seat and in the alleyway and in the corridor and on the mattress. As he returns to his body, he hears the death gasps of past patients. Odor of period pain envelopes the chicken feces. A portrait of the Virgin Mary with her cupped hands looking down at his bare chest.

"Calling Dr. De La Cruz, calling Dr. De La Cruz," Carlita says.

No intercom in that life insurance rent-a-building, just wicked humor amplifying the purple aura following Dr. De La Cruz, decked in a grey graduation robe and chanting omens in dead languages, towering over him. The Doctor stretches out her hand, nails broken with purplish hue on each, but retracts it and instead proffers incisors and green-liquid syringes clustered between her fingers.

"Need to go higher," he says. "Mars is my home."

"Gone, but not entirely," she says with the assurance of her for-profit medical school degree taped to the fridge. "Safe word is papitas."

Wires and tethers marry Sabas to the table. A defibrillator with rat-bitten-wires charges beside him. Numb, he slurps his own tongue, speechless, waiting to fall into the abyss of consciousness. Veins pop, eyes widen. More needles penetrate the skin. Euphoria arouses him. Carlita reaches into his pants, fondles him one last time, steals his wallet.

"Stoner whore," he says.

"I'm a stone, not a gem."

Her edges corrode into a bloom of colors, first red then atomic yellow, as the power of Mexican electricity volts his body upward. He screams, and then another shock reminds him of the goal. Above him Dr. De La Cruz towers holy and haloed, grinning with missing teeth.

"How's it up there?" Dr. De La Cruz asks. "Tell me the real estate rates in Kansas and I'll relocate based on principle."

"He wants to go to Mars," Carlita says.

"All men do. Knows what he wants."

"I want something else," Carlita says. "Something positively unethical. I'll get the keys."

First Sabas sees Dr. De La Cruz's jet-black hair resting on his chest, then he witnesses the sight of her bending over his own body. The two visions fluctuate in his mind, then he sees both simultaneously, then a vague sense of separation emerges until the women's chit-chat misses the divorce. Now, turbo — rolling, skirting, burning, the spirit jets past sky-highways over the heads of unsuspecting nine-to-fivers as the sigh of a razorblade cuts the sky. There, the wheel of torpor encrusted with the hardened sweat of field workers spins with the wind of the flight. Gotta move the wheel of torpor, gotta move the wheel right round by gliding over oceans, through walls, under buildings, kissing lightning as it flashes the open world and riding the ozone rims upward.

No darkness, just blankness. No Chicano vibes, just the self. No logic, just concentric revolutions around the planets and back. Soon Mars, with its surface of grime, emerges. Closer and closer, Mars exudes a dreadful sight — a scar protrudes from its center, exposing the veins and red, dead skin. No looking away, no escape, no other way — straight through the scar of Mars the spirit flies.

The moment feels infinite. In between somewhere and nowhere. A limbo undefined. A simultaneous ending and beginning. It is a space without space, the only place to find something from nothing. That something is the pinnacle, the point, the ecstasy that marks the moment containing all moments. Eventually, a small dot lines the surface. Unbearably, it draws nearer as if on a conquest — the sun. The familiarity stuns. The heat consumes all until there is no more Mars, no more vision. The pull-back begins. Breath warms the mouth and blood flows under the skin.

And the river ripples. Sabas awakens with his feet, his crotch, his stomach, his face wet. Submerged, he gasps but only swallows. In a frenzy he pushes his body upward, swims to the surface, and hears the Thunderbird roar away. He moans at the waning moon undressing behind clouds of smog and smoke trails in this revolving planet dethroning its night. Disoriented, he wades in the current. He laughs before choosing a riverbank. He climbs onto the country wild and undone, unaware of the Rio Grande dripping off his sun-kissed chest.

(2016)

SUNSET STATION

"Meet me at the Sunset Station. See me at the Sunset Station." That was the mantra, that was the paradox. Anasazi could not see the Sunset Station even if it were in front of him. When Anasazi witnessed a trio of ICE agents chant the mantra and then drop dead, he assumed they had found paradise after mixing his batches of blue with someone else's stolen stash. Throughout the El Paso mountains Anasazi had dispersed the wealth of hallucination to the poor gatekeepers of Texas, making true his everlasting vision of the United States: his victims smoking the kush or shooting the shit, brown-skinned brothers on the same bloody needle thinking themselves alone in the vast Mexican loneliness. And all he had to do was drop bags in front of the watchers who thought no one was watching. The watchers were now the watched, but Anasazi still did not know what they saw in their gone eyes.

He wanted in, so for months he cooked up batches of blue and mixed them with everything he could find, but he only saw stars falling through the Franklin Mountains. No good, no bueno. Like a holiday specter for Border Patrol and coyotes alike, he gave but he did not receive — all his victims recited the motto but never shared where they would go. All they did was die. No matter how many times he tried, he could not join them. Stabbing, falling, no breathing — Anasazi's body always stopped him from moving over the edge, somehow. Whenever the light beckoned him, he opened his eyes yet again to the Franklin Mountains. For most bodies in these mountains, every day was a new excavation into the land burnt, bloody, and overrun with federal agents since the Rio Grande became barren in 2048. Except for those like him, who never died.

Take the elderly Native sitting cross-legged under a cactus, licking a slice of pizza before dawn. That monkish woman was meditative in her lick, slurp, pap pleasure revelry even when Anasazi stabbed her repeatedly. Pools of unlimited blood, yet she never stopped licking the pizza, also infinite. For months he used her as a signpost, knowing he was close to camp when he spotted her and her cactus in the distance. No old love pains in those pale eyes, apparently blind, while Anasazi was hungry to see less and forget much. He was tired of looking beyond the bounds of sun-glassed white men and Southwestern poverty awash in brown. He wanted out so badly he grew to abhor her ritual, questioning neither the origin of the pizza nor the possibility of her everlasting life, but resenting her peaceful state.

"Hey Mountain Mama," he said, wincing at her wincing at his voice. "Seen any migra patos pass by here? Coyotes or crossers?"

No response, just tongue on sauce tantalizing, mesmerizing. The glimmer in her glossed-over eyes reminded Anasazi of his Ma's gaze as she wasted away in the Tohono O'odham Nation, waiting for the end of days in its desert ranges. He was not much different than her now, wandering around El Paso and remembering the dramas of childhood in the trailer park. Natives all addicted to something or another because of the ride-throughs. Out of a fever dream, madmen federal agents on horses carried drugs through his makeshift village, tempting those they could and polluting water sources when they couldn't. The worst memory wasn't the perception of these horsemen as saviors helping the Natives escape their drudgeries, but the trauma begetting trauma that eventually got him. The drugs injected by Ma in his sleep were not for fever, as they claimed. The drugs infected his subconscious, and he was never the same.

Now it was the sound of Mountain Mama's rattlesnake tongue and the sight of sacred pizza that triggered Anasazi. He saw his never-ending life centered on kicks tethered to her eternal life, the goddess of the mountains stuck in a loop. Perhaps she too had a place in mind where she could not arrive. Someone had to break the cycle — he snatched the slice from her scaly hands.

"Aha me a riza down in down," she said, calmly. "Aha me a riza down in down."

Anasazi ate the entire slice crust first, wondering if the pizza would multiply inside his stomach and finally kill him. As recompense, he unloaded his backpack full of speed and bliss and tossed stashes around the cactus. As he scattered the Ziploc bags, the early morning sun shone dizzying light on his face. Sweat beads and trembles, and then zoomed out visions from across the Southwest: Everywhere were electric eyes in the copters, and drones above the flaming earth followed intruders and traitors pigmented with borderlands tans. In the distance, strangers in their own land with fence wire in hand. Card players out of Juárez in green-slash trucks. Bandits on the prowl. The gaze of the country averted by the next oil pipeline.

The visions jarred him. It was then he saw drug abuse transform into drug-seductions in school hallways, governors' mansions, hospital bathrooms. It was not unique to him to spread the beauty of tuning out of time and space, yet he considered it the only thing he could do. It would be quite a sight, he thought, to transform this Buddha-like figure into his drug-addled Eve. Yes, with pleasure he would witness his victim give into paradise. It was the only thing he could be expected to do after the horsemen did the same to his people. Meet me at the Sunset Station. See me at the Sunset Station. But he knew not where to go or to look.

After Mountain Mama's chant grew mute, Anasazi climbed a nearby peak to witness her give into temptation. For an hour, it was all sunshine and squints forming his wrinkles faster than the minutes it took for the shadowed figures to emerge from the nearby slope. Even from afar he could spot their drooping double chins and dig-dug fingers and dreadlocks done-over with dirt. Their faces were nondescript, the only defining feature was their sunglassed-eyes imitating Border Patrol agents. Anasazi speculated they were Border

Patrol, maybe those who were fired with pensions revoked, but an otherworldly aura surrounded them. There was an underground beat to their movement — heads bowed to the earth, gangrene-colored clothes hanging off their bodies, boots clinking together — as their handfuls of dust mixed with the stashes. Over a dozen scavengers retrieved the rainbow colors in a sad dash; one minute later they had returned below to get high.

Anasazi took that personally. Stealing his stashes betrayed that unspoken agreement. He didn't mind them, just as he didn't mind the myriad federal agents that littered the mountains, but all he wanted to do was get people high as hell before dying and see what they saw. Before Anasazi could find their footprints, two creatures flittered back over the slope and approached Mountain Mama. They picked her up and fled back underground.

When he descended, the stashes were gone save one baby blue mix occupying Mountain Mama's former spot. Had they really abducted an unsuspecting old woman? Was he next?

A shadow crept along the burning brush and dust, accompanied by crunching footsteps. Anasazi dove toward the slope, and having underestimated its steepness, tumbled down until he clutched the bare earth. He climbed to witness a creature sampling his stash. Silent and still, he stared at the body snorting his speed and contorting after several whiffs. He unmade the creature convulsing before him. It made him smile.

"Meet me at the Sunset Station. See me at the Sunset Station," the creature said, its voice croaking each syllable as if it were already dead.

There it was. Suddenly, the world was a trailer park once more. What Anasazi witnessed now triggered those childhood memories of blank stares and mindless mouth gaping. All that was old became new again: escaping CPS abductions, squeezing an agent's jugular, cooking products in desolation shacks. Whatever this creature saw before its eyes, Anasazi wanted it — it was the only way out.

He dashed up the slope, his breathing so intense it caught the attention of the creature still enraptured by the mantra. Half-alerted and half-delusional, the creature stumbled away at half the speed of its earlier cohort — which was still alarmingly fast to Anasazi, who struggled to keep up with it as it galloped on all fours like a wild beast. If it were not for its drug-induced meanderings, Anasazi would have missed it digging furiously at the ground where his cohort had emerged. There was nothing there for a minute, and Anasazi would have pounced if suddenly a hole did not open in the earth so quickly and so large it consumed the creature. Dumbfounded, Anasazi jumped into the shrinking hole as the surrounding dirt closed it in, hiding it from view forever.

It was a long fall with seemingly no end. Eventually, Anasazi righted himself as if sinking into the darkness with no light in sight. He assumed he had stopped falling, although he could not feel any ground below him. Neither could he sense the space around him, and he wondered if the earth would close on top of him or if he would fall through to the other side of the world. In any case, it was a welcome change of pace. Soon, Anasazi heard a squeal tearing through the space. Then a tremendous swarm of red eyes, hundreds, surrounded him. All out of rhythm they blinked rapidly, switching on and off his only light source. Looking into them only worsened his headache.

"Okay bastards, stop the freakshow," he said. "Give me the one who snorted my blue shit and saw the Sunset Station."

He felt poking on his left knee. Mountain Mama sat cross-legged next to him, and the roar of Anasazi's wail was swallowed by her booming voice chanting, Aha me a riza down in down.

Like the flick of a switch, the space became inverted. Black turned to white, and all the red eyes morphed into a single creature wearing its Border Patrol sunglasses chanting, Meet me at the Sunset Station. See me at the Sunset Station.

"Señor Montemayor! Pleasure to make your acquaintance again," Anasazi said as he approached the creature and grasped its temples. "Tell me what you saw."

Montemayor likewise grabbed Anasazi, sinking its sharp fingernails into his eye sockets and crushing his face between his behemoth hands. A muffled laugh sounded through the grip, boldly inviting yet another attempt at taking Anasazi's life. The intensity of their death-grips shook both of their bodies, and Montemayor's face trembled so heavily that its sunglasses began to slip. The eyes were not glaring red — they were the same as Mountain Mama's pale eyes, if not the very same eyes transplanted onto its face. But Anasazi saw the difference. He saw himself in that gaze, red dripping from his own eyes in streams of blood. Eventually, red consumed his vision just as the dirt had filled in the hole. He let go of Montemayor and wiped his face, but the red would not fall from his eyes. He could not feel his eyes.

Slowly, forms appeared before him: familiar sky, ground, trailers, shacks, people. The smell of overcooked batches, the feeling of soft dirt underneath his floppy shoes. He was home as he had always remembered it, and it made him angry. He could still hear Mountain Mama chanting, but as a faraway echo. He could not see her. Wherever Anasazi looked, Montemayor stood, watching. When he marched toward it, it reappeared farther away, watching. Focusing on a faraway Baboquivari peak, he witnessed the Montemayor morph into view, watching. Looking into the palm of his hand, he saw the shrunken Montemayor looking up at him, watching. No one around him seemed to mind the watching. In fact, when Anasazi approached his neighbors and childhood friends, they merely watched him along with Montemayor. No shock, no acknowledgement. They blankly stared straight through him.

"I didn't ask for purgatory," Anasazi said, pointing to Montemayor. "Either you take me to the Sunset Station, or you kill me all the way to hell. Not this shit."

Montemayor lifted its arm and pointed with two fingers behind Anasazi. When he turned around, he saw the Montemayor holding open the door to a trailer with an American flag covering the window. The sight froze him in place. His Ma and Pa stepped outside, clearly high as hell, and walked toward him. He could feel nails clawing into his back, hard slaps across his face, the needle piercing his arm — the pain and pleasure fusing. With every step they drew closer, and after a lifetime of ruminating on those moments he could think of nothing to do now. He opened his mouth — I'm your son, not a goddamn experiment! — but the words did not sound. Anasazi tensed his body as his parents approached, but they walked past him.

Turning, he witnessed the entire trailer park walk away in droves toward the desert. Montemayor stood in the center of it all, beckoning Anasazi to follow. How long he walked, Anasazi could not begin to guess. His body did not feel fatigued despite the burning sun and heavy sand. No one stopped. No one spoke. No one turned. He simply followed them for what seemed like an eternity, his gaze piercing the backs of his parents all the while. It comforted him to see them facing away. They did indeed exist outside the village, away from the horsemen's gaze. Throughout this self-imposed exodus, he wondered if that was all that was left — existing. Alive, but not living. Part of the group, but alone. Watching, but not seeing.

Eventually, Anasazi realized they were arriving somewhere as he heard Mountain Mama's chant sound louder. Then, it suddenly stopped. Soon, the more familiar sights of the Franklin Mountains emerged, and he saw her sitting beneath her cactus. The crowd formed a wide circle around Mountain Mama, facing her as they stood side-by-side.

"You think you can break me?" Anasazi asked, feeling a vague sense of déjà vu as Mountain Mama licked her pizza. "If you freaks can take the memories out of my head, you can take the Sunset Station out of the Montemayor."

Montemayor stood next to Mountain Mama, pointing toward the horizon. Horses neighed in the distance. Galloping around the circle, the horsemen surveyed the Natives. No badges to be seen, just black robes bearing the acronym ICE on the backs.

One woman rode her horse into the circle and towered over Anasazi, blocking the sun. "We've been waiting."

When she rode away and the sun shone again, the horsemen were already in motion. Swiftly, the horsemen bestowed on their victims stashes of drugs, syringes, and other gifts that compelled them to dance, jump, flex — every single person in a mad frenzy. As if a silent song had enraptured them, they circled Mountain Mama, Montemayor, and Anasazi. The circle rotated faster and faster counterclockwise, and Anasazi had no choice but to stare at the despair masked by ecstasy. Ma and Pa pushed each other's backs, tumbling over themselves when they took turns. Goofy faces, thrusting pelvises, flailing arms. Everyone letting loose their bodies.

Eventually, the horsemen dismounted and joined along, sprinkling substances on their tongues as they hopped with the rhythm.

Anasazi sat next to Mountain Mama, head in hands. At first, the silence provided reprieve from facing the horror of his sick pleasures turned against him, but he could no longer look away when the villagers and ICE agents began to chant: Meet me at the Sunset Station. See me at the Sunset Station.

(2020)

AFTER THE WALL

Running along the Rio Grande River is like feeling the weight of the country pushing and pulling my body across a house without walls. Of course, there really is a wall and everyone knows the river will swallow it eventually, but long-distance running has become too lonely to ignore how neither country cares to bring me home unless it's lonely too. Feeling bordered, stuck between two steel tormentors grating against one another to forge no-man's land, and the heat is closing in. So hot that my cross-country team stopped running. It wasn't the election; it was the long run toward it. On my last run, I could sense it: the creeping feeling of having lost something followed me like a shrouded stranger, a specter of the old miles.

Humidity hiding in shacks long abandoned, flatland horizons yawning light over the Rio Grande Valley, silence balanced on the edge of grass blades brown and brittle. It was all there, untouched, and that was the beauty of running with my hips swaying to the rhythm of the borderland morning: slow and calm and full of time. How many miles were left after the wall, I could never count. I just ran at the bottom, to the bottom of the country past the ancient Santa Ana Wildlife Refuge. It was hard to forget those cross-country days, but now to run was to forget the trails we once conquered. Back then, the world was wherever our legs and lungs could take us, and we rarely looked beyond our next mile. Dead dads, three-dollars-a-day meals, expired papers, no matter — we sizzled on the roads, we cut through the canals.

But after the wall, we lost something. Last I heard, Russian was in graduate school up north solving climate change and chasing his "black queens." Danny Bear changing oil in Monterrey, Julian selling it in Houston. Beans overdosed. And Josh sitting in his border patrol truck always parked at the old Santa Ana Wildlife Refuge canal entranceway, waving at me as I passed. Today his window was up, but no wave. I recognized his number, K96269, embedded in green above his right tire, remembering how he would say, "I'm not a number. I'm just a man," when asked if he was third or fourth man on the team. In my hurry, although I don't remember what I was rushing toward, I pretended to forget about the truck until the engine started and it drove alongside me.

"Tommy Gunn, you've gotten so brown I thought you were a beaner," Josh said.

"Just testing you, you know."

I slowed down with the truck, which swung in front of me before Josh parked and stumbled out. Green uniform and everything, but still the same lanky fronterizo: head tilted low with a knock-knee gait. Whiter skin than mine. I embraced him for the first time in years.

"What are you doing down here?" he asked.

"Just running."

"I heard about your campaign. Running the country yet?"

"Just through it. Breaking through power isn't done in a day."

"All you do is run. Ever think about running away from the Valley for once?"

I almost laughed — the only place for me is the borderlands where my blood is always warm.

"Someday," I said.

"Me too, man. I hope so too."

The pain behind every word was not like the rush of deoxygenated blood rushing to and from the brain, but the exertion of reaching a finish line obscured by hands and shouts and incense. You could pass through and everyone turned away, thinking you were done, but you knew the running would never end. Despite all the miles, all the hills and rivers and streets I passed, every climb and fall, each step and breath pouring out of me back into the shared space Josh and I occupied whether we were together in the pack or separated by place, we had never arrived. Here we were, chasing shadows. Myself outspent ten-to-one by a GEO Group Democrat while Josh's trademark Garmin was gone, traded in for a badge and paycheck. Or worse, pawned and forgotten. I couldn't ask.

"You know, patrolling can get pretty boring. It's eighty percent waiting and twenty percent watching for illegals," he said.

"Ever get lonely?"

"Nah, the boys bullshit over the radio all the time. I mean, even hearing them breathe is sometimes a relief. Like when we used to run in a pack."

"Pain feels better with a team."

"Man, I see that out here all the time."

The heat of blood was still coursing through me, infecting my limbs with the runner's dance: twitching and jumping in place, arms akimbo. It seemed amusing to Josh, who had long forgotten the runner's necessity to go, go, go. The wall's shade was shrinking, and I almost leaned up against it. But he just stood there, his sunglass eyes round and dark against his reddened face, searching for something to say. He opened his mouth, but a westerly wind blew, and he remained silent rather than try to talk above the noise. Was the specter watching us now? Perhaps it would cut in between us, whisking away our awkwardness and returning our adolescent handshakes and towel-slaps. Maybe it would even take us away.

"So, I heard this wall is taking away your job," I said, almost yelling.

"That's what Washington likes to hear."

"Remember Jesse?"

"Who?"

"Remember when we were doing the easy twelve through the refuge and we found a teenager who had just crossed the river? And he ran with us like he was our teammate. He even ran ahead of the whole pack. I tried catching him, but he was too fast. Then he jumped over the Santa Ana fence and zoomed by Coach Austin."

"Can you repeat that? Wind was in my ears."

"The immigrant who ran with us out of Santa Ana, where the old routes were."

"Oh yeah, didn't that fat patrolman get her once she crossed the road?"

"What? No, that didn't happen. It was a guy."

"Pretty sure it did, Tommy."

"You're confusing him with someone else."

"Maybe I just remember it differently."

"Well, I bet he could jump this."

Where the winds blow, that's where Jesse will go, I often thought. Somewhere out there running like a Road King, or maybe writing the next Great American Novel. Providing for a family, or living alone in the mountains, or managing a city. Searching for more routes unencumbered. Jesse made me think: Where do I want to be when the running ends? Wherever Jesse ended up. What's running without the thrill of having a chaser breathing on your shoulder, the straggler using you to rev on, you afraid to look back and hoping the always-onward path ends somewhere soon so you can turn and realize there was nobody there except you?

"Hey Tommy, I stopped you for a reason. I need to tell you something."

"Anything."

"I'm just following orders. I got a call from HQ. They don't want people running along the wall anymore."

It seemed like the wind had hit the wall. It boomed, like during early morning runs where everyone's breath is sleepy and tired but yours is so alive that it's the only sound you can hear for miles except no one hears it but you. I shifted in place, changing the flow of my dance to one with heaviness on my head, on my shoulders, on my back.

"I mean, it's the closest thing to the old routes that we've got," I said.

"Yeah, but they're gone now."

"You say that like it doesn't matter. Those were our routes."

"Look, I wasn't for the wall, but it's here now. So, we live with it."

"I haven't seen the river in years."

"It's still there. I keep it safe."

"Well, you're the wall watcher. Let me through every once and a while, will you?"

"If I want to lose my job."

Josh extended his hand, and I shook it. That was all we did because there was nothing left to say. He revved his engine and drove away.

Then I ran after the truck. Pushing, pumping, propelling all my force forward as if I were now the chaser to Josh's long-lost self-searching for something real. But Josh sped on, and the roar of his engine seemed to shake the wall and the cold-hearted earth and my own heart. I smiled like Jesse would have, running faster and faster after the green slash. I didn't know why. I just knew it was another run and surely it meant something. But soon my chest heaved, and I knew I would hit the wall either figuratively or literally. When Josh slowed down, the squeal from his wheels frightened a flock of birds perched on the ledge. Off they went into Mexico, and their shadows fell before my face as I blinked and breathed at the same time, questioning my actions yet continuing my mad dash when Josh leaned out the window and motioned me to hurry. Hurry where? I knew could go everywhere, but it felt like I was left with nowhere.

The brush burned under Josh's tires, and the sun kissed my neck turning to witness him rush past me. I chased him again, and he repeated himself. Again, and again. The hopeless loop.

"Tired yet?" he asked, looking down at me from his seat.

Inhaling his exhaust, I squatted close to the ground. My legs shook. My temples pounded, cold sweat dripping onto my lips bitten, almost bloody. The shade of his truck hid me from the rest of the Valley until he drove closer to the entranceway: an eyesore of vertical wooden planks attached to sliders at the top and bottom. When he stepped out, he looked at me the way he used to look at the pack quickening its pace. Raised eyebrows, mouth hung open. Ready to run toward something because someone else was catching up.

"I'm not doing this again, so don't tell anyone," he said, reaching into his shirt.

Behind his sunglasses, I saw closed eyes. A slight smile curved inward, suppressing itself. He pulled out a card to swipe on a nearby kiosk. The door began to slide apart.

His patronizing hand gestures beckoning me to follow, Josh jumped back in and opened the passenger door. But I took my time staring at the old new world. It was as if desert mirages could burn eyes. A burst of humidity slammed against my face, forcing me to squint at the nothingness. No more trees and no more trails, just a makeshift road winding into the river over a mile away. From afar, it seemed all roads ended at the river sloping onto the banks of Mexico, still green with trees and shrubbery.

Although my body chilled against the dark side of the wall, I cooked inside Josh's patrol truck. Our forged space could not compare. Into the Southmost South we went, A pair of former teammates going our own way into a burning third world. Bordered and fragmented and melting. We parked beside the river.

"What did you want to see?" Josh asked.

"There's not much."

"Yeah, not anymore."

I glanced at Josh, who tapped his fingers on the wheel in an inconsistent jitter. His eyes darted every which way while his head seemed locked downward. As he shifted in his seat, I imagined asking him about the old days. If he too had missed something as he absorbed the immensity of the dirt and the sky and his riverbank-sunrise-flatland-job-musings. If he had ever felt followed by the specter, watching him as he chased after unwitting immigrants, his light skin overshadowed by a ghost light in the dark. I wondered if he too could feel an impending presence looming over us, welcoming us into the fray.

"What do you call this place between the wall and the river?" I asked instead.

"No-man's land."

I got out and ran away — stepping onto the well-worn paths, circling around an invisible circuit-way with the wind bouncing northbound and back in a volley — expecting to finally get caught, or perhaps catch the force pushing me on and on. Dust kicked up. Musty odor. Fumes from Josh's truck trailed behind me. The wheels rolled over my footprints. If I slowed down, his bumper chilled my hamstrings. If I sprinted, he caught up to my heels.

"Just like old times," Josh said after a whooping laugh. "Don't expect me to follow without my A/C, though."

To this day, I don't know what triggered the urge to sit back inside Josh's truck besides the gnawing feeling that I had reached the end and it was not what I had expected. 'Round and 'round I ran until I was out of space. There was so much more beyond and behind me, but I stopped. I had expected to arrive, but not to stop. I had become neither the followed nor the chaser but rather someone in between, waiting for whomever come who may as I made my own way. But I was not where I wanted to be, and I did not know where that was, and I did not know how to find it yet. And so, I completed my last run.

"Well, what do you think, Congressman?" Josh asked.

"I shouldn't have crossed. Nothing is the same."

Josh offered me a silent ride back to town, but I declined. We entered Texas and he drove down the wall, clouding his truck in dust. I walked home, thinking: Here's to you, borderlands, whose runaway long-distance runner has run out of shadows and exposed himself to the desolation hiding behind it all, and even your border needs a border as you crawl north, never north enough. And I still wondered where Jesse had ended up.

(2017)

I Know I Will Be Leaving Here

I'm detained in the border patrol nation of Texas, cursed by my brother's skin shaded bastard-white from all the deportations he's done. But who am I to talk shit? Maybe I just threw away the real reason I'm here. Slippery memory is a thing — it's what we cling to when locked up in a room with the square feet of a two-stepper. I say we assuming other people know what I mean by getting detained so long I don't know how much longer I'll remember all this. Everyone knows the borderlands brings the heat like it's no one's business, but it's this idea of business that's melting my brain to the point where the past and the present mesh into one long memory. I know why they're holding me here. To think that these bastards are making more money off my body than I ever did making beds at motels. And for what? Sitting around and getting watched.

That's the thing about living on the border — you're always looked at. Well, at least people like me: diabetic, hunchback, morena. Add a Guadalajara accent and you've got border patrol pulling reasonable suspicions out of their ass. Even when they're not around I feel the weight of their eyes lurking around the corner. That too-clean-looking car driving slowly down the side-street, the güero standing still by the vocational school. I could feel the heat closing in long before my detainment.

Look, I'm illegal and I know it. Pity me all you want, but there's something about being an outlaw in Texas. It's like I'm on the run every second, that cross etched into Mount Cristo following my every move, giving away my location. El Paso even looks like goddamn El Topo. But I never worried much because of my younger brother. Bobby joined the border patrol when he was 32, tired of parking people's cars for a living and terrified of a mid-life crisis. Unlike me, he was born on the right side of the border and looks like it — a 21st-century desperado peeling tires, not caring about the earth devouring him. All that driving was good practice for catching illegals. You know that scene in *The Catcher in the Rye* where Holden catches all the kids falling off the cliff — Bobby wanted to do that but with illegals. Bobby once said when you witness a deportation, you expect to see one of three faces: I'm coming back you know, shit how do I come back, and I have no idea where I'm going tonight. It made me wonder which one I did when the agent cuffed me since I knew he knew migration never ends.

Bobby and I used to be tight before he got me detained. It started with an innocent question: When are you driving again? When 2017 came around, I couldn't even drive myself to work anymore — you can imagine getting to and from the Motel 6 off the 10 is real hell when border patrol starts acting like state troopers. For over a goddamn year I walked, crunching plastic water bottles down my ass to keep cool, and Bobby never knew until he saw me cut across the Whataburger parking lot. I mean, how else was I getting to work? No fat jokes but walking sucks — everything looks the same for too long and by the time you reach the other side of a building your attention's on the vato walking too slowly in front of you. Life's different when you're not seeing things from a moving car.

Bobby wouldn't let me move until I answered his question. Mind you he's in his border patrol car asking me a question in front of a drive-through, people eating their fries like popcorn. It just pissed me off — it's always a spectacle with him. It wasn't 9/11 that got him screwed up. It was just too much *Cops*. The deportation game is the chase and thrill, and you can't say anything to Bobby to turn off his intensity until the brown people are taken off screen for good. But for the people watching reality, there's no forgetting the scene — no reshoots and there's no next time exactly like this time — and you'd be surprised to find someone other than Bobby who still believed that brown skin did not belong on camera.

I'm not the white man's burden, I said. I'm not white, he said. Yeah, just a bastard. Forgot whether I told him that last part or not.

Bobby bit his lower lip as if imagining a world where we could both talk about a mutual mother. I felt like I had finally won, but when arguing with someone inside a car only the driver wins because he can end it all in a second. The wheel was power. I remembered the slide — the letting go of a tightly-wound-wheel and the whole two tons turning with me. Sweeter than the loneliness of womanhood and faster than the bastardization of siblinghood. I watched Bobby's hands, but he just clenched the wheel until his fingers were actually white. I swung the door open before he could finish parking. Before I could cross my arms, he caught my wrist like I just rose from the Rio.

Respect it, Mari, he said. I'm doing this because I love you. I could get fired you know. But I'm the man of the family now.

When he released me, my skin looked like his until the blood rushed back. I winced only to prove that I was the human. All the way to the motel, the sound of Bobby's engine stuck with me. Old, government-funded, distinctly manly. Something about how his foot pushed on the pedal must have infected the soundwaves. After he dropped me off, I heard his car roar away into who-knows-where, limited within the eight-hour span he had until he needed to pick me up again, but the heat remained. Hot and burning, urging me to move, move.

So, Bobby started driving me to work without telling anybody. Demagnetizes the magnet, he said, exposing all that pocho in his eyes, some sort of hazel from neither Mom nor Dad, which could never see enough, absorb enough, dig enough while on the road. To think I used to love driving around with him. Back then, the world was wheels. Those tires and all the roads ahead and everywhere and everything was ours. From the Tohono reservation to Rio Grande City, we knew the border better than anyone else — all the desert horizons and beat mountains were like memories rolling under our wheels. The vibrating seat almost catching fire from engine overload, the air condition revving the heat of blood down my arms, the wavy vistas telling me that I was more than an illegal. But now Bobby and I couldn't forget that last part. Driving me around was part of his mission, and I was reminded every day how fortunate I was to benefit from his job.

Ironically enough, on the day it happened I mentioned how I hated watching Mexicans pass by because I felt like I was ratting them out. He told me, You should be grateful you're invisible.

You know that feeling of driving on the expressway so fast it feels like you're invisible? It sounds dumb but the feeling is real — speed is cover. Drivers see you pass, but by the time they shake their head you're already off the next exit. They see the green Thunderbird, not a brown thunder-cunt — I learned that one from Bobby. Yeah, that's what these checkpoints were designed to stop. In cities like El Paso where Spanish is flung like rocks across the expressway, border patrol agents materialize on the other side to throw them back. That's what it felt like as we slowed down to wait in line for one of Bobby's buddies to pass us through.

Act natural, he said. A que no. Like there was something natural about driving around in a border patrol car with your border patrol brother and getting questioned by border patrol in the middle of the street. I was even thinking why Bobby had to stop in the first place, and maybe he didn't have to, but he did anyway like a good ol' boy. And to think the first thing his bastard buddy asked him was, Where'd you nab her? Chingao. Here's another thing about Bobby —

it's never simple. Like he always has to go with the flow. He never stops and starts again, reverses or turns around — it's always about outmaneuvering an imaginary enemy that's usually himself. And so, he responded, She was lost, and I saved her.

"Lost" makes you think I was wandering somewhere and then misplaced my means of mobility like a dope, but nope, I lost myself right there, the moment Bobby turned El Paso whiter than the border patrol agent's laugh into the car. So lost she crossed the border! the agent yelled. Yeah, she'd be dead without me, was all Bobby said.

My ears were already eating sound bites from the radio reporting on New Mexico militiamen. Now this bullshit. Where's the lie, Mari! Bobby's face said. To anyone who looks like me, these encounters are always a balancing act on a razor's edge, and I felt dizzy as if I knew something bad was gonna happen, something escaping to the surface of my skin like rising humidity. And once I saw those bubbles ripple across my arms, my trembling hands flicked them both off hard — harder than how hard they worked scrubbing toilets.

That was either suspicious or endearing. Either way, it made him, Isaac I later learned, hang back a little, rocking on his heels. Something about that tilt turned me off. There's a half-mile of vehicles behind us, too afraid to honk but not patient enough to turn their engines off. Wherever they were going, they were now part of Isaac's power trip. I guess the combination of July heat, engine fumes, and toxic machismo made him decide to call over his buddy waiting in a car across the street.

Hey, mind if I jump in with you, Bobby? Isaac asked. My shift's almost over. You're going to the station, right?

Bobby knew North wasn't East. Bobby knew anything he said would be used against him. Bobby knew Isaac wanted to watch me get booked. He nodded his pretty little head. Good little güero helping out. And there I was with palms on thighs, stiffer than on a January midnight. No sweat, just trembles and accelerated wrinkling as I watched Bobby turning and turning, the wheel sliding slick through his hands with his kneecap as the buffer, stopping the car from crashing into the others. Out of the line and into southbound traffic, he let the windows down, feeling the wind blow against that bald head blocking the mid-afternoon sun.

This was Isaac's ride. I could tell by the way Bobby jerked from lane to lane, suddenly following the speed limit. I had never seen his jaw clenched like that, like he was chewing something to death. In the rearview mirror, Isaac smiled like a saint, probably realizing how something's off and he's got Bobby by the balls. That's machistas in a nutshell — they don't know the thing itself, just the significance of the thing.

You speak English? Isaac asked me. I heard the way he said it, not the words themselves, like some sort of exterminator surveying the territory, listening for insect screams. The engine seemed to quiet down, waiting for my response: Nah.

Bobby coughed, then Isaac chuckled. Bobby swerved the roads leading zigzag toward the border patrol station, his speed making the silence slower, more intense. The see-nothing horizon outside looked the same and we remained the same inside. Every minute was a confined jam. Isaac and his vizor-reliant brain, Bobby and his go, go, go. I was just the brown burden. I guess there was something empowering about re-magnetizing my magnet, but I felt nothing.

Soon we turned into the parking lot. Isaac shifted comfortably in his seat, taking up more space with his arms outstretched like we had entered his country now, but then hurried outside once we parked.

See ya inside, amigos, Isaac said before tapping the window and waving two fluffy fingers toward us.

The last time I saw Bobby, he was crying. But here's the thing: I know it was because Isaac treated him like a little bitch. Don't give me that change-of-heart shtick. Bobby's final words were all I needed to know I need to do my job, Mari. They're watching me.

You, whoever reads this, especially if it's Bobby, let me tell you sitting in a cell ain't shit compared to what goes on outside. Every day, you get the feeling you're being watched by these devil-dog seat-warmers every time you walk out with more than $10 worth of tiendita shit. If it's a Tuesday and you get the chocolate protein shake with five lottos for luck, you feel like a real chingona until the truck with the green stripe starts up and follows you down the side street. No, not la migra — just some asshole with a green-striped truck. But you never know, and so you walk like all those white people in the 80s action movies. At least in here you can see the security camera. And they gave me paper and a pen, so you forget about it for a while.

If this year's taught me anything, it's that people named Bob aren't going to save the country. Whether I'm deported or not, I know my way around. And maybe I won't come back. I remember what Dad said about the vatos in Nogales: no gas, no vas. Just pass them by. Who knows if we would have reached the border if we had stopped for them. That's the paradox of a rearview mirror. You can always see what you've left behind even after it's gone.

(2018)

A SOUTH TEXAS SEPTEMBER

A South Texas September is hard to accept, but I learned to laugh at change at a young age. To a five-year-old boy, summertime never ends because the palm trees remain bare and bent, heatwaves and humidity float effortlessly from the Gulf, and swimming pools stay open until sundown. But the school bus that passed by my barrio every morning at 7:15 AM reminded me of where I stood in time. Unaware of responsibility, except for turning off the TV after leaving the living room, I wondered why the older boys and girls would wait by the street sign to board that monster vehicle, rivaled only by my uncle's eighteen-wheeler. I made it my ritual to stand by the mailbox and watch the brown faces stare at me as the bus whizzed by, heading somewhere. I never rode that bus. Weeks passed until I learned I would be headed down the street in a different vehicle to a different school.

Now 7:15 AM meant that Aunt Aurora's red pick-up truck would take Grandma and me to Faith Christian School. It was only a mile away, but it was another world bereft of brownness and familiarity. Grandma, a dark-skinned migrant Mexicana who knew the taste of sweat, looked out of place among the suited white men and dressed women hugging their children on the first day of school. It was as if a mirror reflected an unflattering image back to me. I was white, they were white, but nothing felt right. I had no reason to feel uncomfortable, except for the fact that the only white man I had ever seen was Batman after taking off his mask. I never knew my white Dad, and my Mom's light-brown skin had never led me to question why I looked differently than everyone around me.

But now whiteness, tall and imposing, surrounded me as I held Grandma's hand before entering my kindergarten classroom. Only five small bodies occupied the long table in the center of the room decorated with rainbows, monosyllabic encouragements, and the first hundred numbers that would become our mantra. They all seemed timid, unaware of how to act in front of their parents and peers in the same space. Hesitant, I gripped Grandma's wrinkles until she dragged me inside. Entering the room meant joining a social sphere that judged solely on sight, and when the crowd saw a brown-skinned woman with a tiny white boy, looks of pity projected from their eyes. Some faces contorted, seemingly discomforted by this incongruent portrait of brownness and whiteness. Their thought bubbles roamed across the room's sky-blue ceiling like clouds, and they must have contained tales of highly paid caretakers, abandoned parents, and misplaced Winter Texans.

Cutting through the fantasies no doubt unraveling in everyone's minds, the lone Mexican woman in the room approached us, eager to shake our hands. She introduced herself as Mrs. Batres, and as everyone would later call her: Mrs. B. My five-year-old mind didn't know at that moment that we had met the only certified teacher at the school. She was just a reassuring brown face, like Mom and Grandma.

Soon, I was torn away from the scene and forced to join the table of strangers. They sat silent and embarrassed, brimming with youthful vigor but restricted by the dreaded classroom seats with invisible restraints. Khaki pants, ankle-length skirts, and ties covered us like costumed posterchildren for uniform expression. No smiles on those faces, no reflection in those brains, no future in those eyes, just sitting in the present moment. Finally, I met other children my age, a reality I had only known watching family sitcoms. Now real children sat in front of me, seemingly interested in making friends. One scrawny and red-faced child approached me with a smile.

"The doubter," Kyle said after learning my name.

I had no clue what he meant at the time because religion had not yet infiltrated my consciousness, nor did I realize that I had been enrolled at a Christian school. After all the parents left and Mrs. B assumed her authority over the classroom, she taught us the concept of prayer — "the best way to start off the day" — and how it could make me a better person. All eyes were closed, and heads bowed, except mine. These concentrated believers congregated into a classroom with the United States and Texas flags flanking the corners of the chalkboard, and where was I? Lost in the space between reality and the mental space everyone else found themselves in, speaking with the divine, while I sat dumbfounded and confused.

"Amen!"

Amen, I repeated, not knowing the word's meaning or significance. But since Mrs. B said it, I said it too. If Mrs. B rose her hand, I rose my hand. If Mrs. B smiled, I smiled. My first day passed in a blur of mindless imitation until lunch, and even then, I watched for Mrs. B's signals. Instinctively, I listened to the brown woman, as I had all my life up to that point, while feeling alienated from many of my white peers. It seemed like only I shared the same enthusiasm for listening to Mrs. B — they yelled and littered during lunch, yelped during recess, and poked each other before the dismissal bell rang. By then, Kyle had forgotten my name, and he soon became just another face in the crowd of students scurrying to their parents' vehicles.

One mile later, I cared only about being in my Mom's arms. Exhausted after supervising convenience stores in Mexico all day, she arrived home soon after I returned, excited about what I considered an uneventful day. Out of all the events and words that flashed before my mind, I focused on one: the prayer.

"I'm happy they're teaching you how to pray," Mom said, satisfied.

Despite her answer, I felt an uncontrollable urge to ask the question. For nine hours, I had surrounded myself with people who looked like me. Yet, in my mind they were inherently different.

"Why do I look so different than you?" I asked Mom.

The question confused her. I stroked my forearm, as if besmirched. Grandma, overhearing the question above the cooking quesadillas in the kitchen, chuckled and stood beside Mom in solidarity. Suffocating fumes infused with a delicious aroma. Agitated, I squirmed on the sofa, waiting for a response.

"Well, your dad is white, and I'm brown, and you just happened to come out white!"

Mom and Grandma laughed, melting away the tension, and even I joined in the chorus. But I had no reason to laugh — I did it because it felt right, like it was expected. Still empty, still not understanding, I took my seat at the kitchen table and waited for dinner.

"At least you prayed today," Mom said.

From this moment, most of my kindergarten days blur into monotony in my memory. But few scenes stand out. Pastor Meyer would interrupt class from time to time, breaking our cycle of prayer, pledges, penmanship, and play. Pastor Meyer's waxed, bald head would stoop next to mine, investigating my handwriting, proclaiming it "good." On Wednesdays, his sermons would also call the Word "good," using his black wallet as a symbol of religious foundation and fortitude, the money inside inherent corruption (Mom didn't like her tuition money being called sinful), and the palm on which it all rested as god. I liked Wednesday sermons because they got us out of class and extended recess time. Sometimes Pastor Meyer would stomp by the swings and wave his bear-like hands at all the elementary students, reminding everyone to treat fear as mere play, because god was watching over all, even on the playground.

Now Pastor Meyer serves as the ghost in the machine of rhetoric clunking in my brain. He marks my simultaneous beginning and departure from Christianity. I was still a white Mexican, but my acceptance into this insular community relied on ignoring my racial identity and embracing what I considered a constructed ideal of "goodness." Even as a young boy, I knew this by the unprepared sermons, by the blank faces from teachers and church leaders alike, and by the lack of answers to hard questions.

One morning in late September, when I had settled into the rhythm of school, I dared to ask another bold question, this time during our weekly Bible story.

"Why are all the people the same? They are all white."

All of Mrs. B's colorful illustrations contained white men and women who looked entirely different from the people I pictured in my mind while reading the Bible. Naturally, everyone was brown since Mom and Grandma were brown.

"Because the pictures say so!" Kyle said, as if an indescribable anger began to rise from somewhere deep in his body.

Mrs. B seemed both concerned and amused by the question. She looked at Jesus sitting on the Mount and the disciples all blanketed with snow skin.

"Good question. I think the picture people might have gotten it wrong."

But no more — she changed the subject immediately, and I sat at my desk still yearning for a reason. I looked at my fellow classmates, and none of them, especially tiny Kyle, seemed bothered.

Afterward, prayer time made the world dark. By now, I had learned to bow my head and close my eyes, but my inner voice remained silent, and no one else knew but me. The unarticulated questions concerning what would soon become my racial identity and skepticism toward religion floated in my consciousness, waiting to break free in the form of words. But all I could do was imagine myself floating, then falling, then floating, then falling into a white abyss of unknown knowledge. Whiteness, probably from the sunlight piercing through the window, rubbed my eyelids sore. Every second that I stayed squinting, with that pretend prayer face on, I felt as if something or someone would creep up behind me and force my eyes open. No one else in the room could tell because they were all enraptured in their own spirituality, like at the end of Sunday service when everyone would jump to their feet and dance and sing and fling their arms in a frenzy guided by a spirit entering their bodies as if nobody was watching. But now we were all still and silent, still, and silent.

In between the prayer times, I would fail to reach any conclusions about myself. The complexities of being a white Mexican did not trouble me, but they confused me. Everywhere I went, from the local Whataburger to the corner convenience store to the movie theater, everyone was brown. When Mom would take me to work on the weekends, everyone in line at the bridge was brown and everyone at her store was brown. Light brown, dark brown, tanned brown, all shades of a single identity.

But Faith Christian School served as a white bubble that could only be popped by Aunt Aurora's red pick-up truck. Once I entered the bubble, I was surrounded by whiteness until she picked me up again and I returned to the world of Pharr, Texas, where 95% of the residents proudly deemed themselves Mexicans, touting their skin as a form of documentation. The fact that I was white, and therefore part of the prevailing Faith Christian School student body, never struck me. I recognized my whiteness, but I did not feel white. Being white meant having the best lunch boxes and newest candies. Being white meant getting dropped off in fancy cars and picked up by parents dressed in clothes that were nearly as expensive. Being white meant being the opposite of Mexican. I was Mexican; therefore, I could not have been white.

Although I was raised by brown-skinned Mexicans, even my interests seemed to diverge from the expected cultural norms. I knew nothing about Spanish. Mom intentionally taught me English first, ensuring that I would not fall into the gap of not knowing either language, as she had endured as a child. Neither the school nor Mom could force me to eat beans and brown rice, and the only good taco was a cheese taco. Every morning, Mom cranked corridos on the radio until I opened the door, disgusted, and gratefully left that world behind. But despite her efforts, I found myself in an in-between state. Stuck between my culture and skin color, I was walking the tight rope of identity with razor blades cutting off the ends. I needed to run toward a side or fall to my inevitable doom of never truly knowing myself. At the time, considering myself a Mexican boy and a white boy would mean balancing both lifestyles, something I failed to do. I implicitly knew this when I would sit by Grandma during her Univision and telenovela marathons, all while I urged her to change the channel so I could watch Pokémon.

Believe it or not, Pokémon became the grounds of warfare between the school and Mom. My passion for the TV show, the video games, and the card game had resulted in a Pokémon-themed birthday party. Determined to make it memorable, Mom convinced Mrs. B to hold the party during lunch in my classroom. Never before had the classroom looked so colorful and happy. Creatures colored yellow, red, blue, and every combination of shades and hues imaginable aligned the walls and hung from the ceiling, and their smiling faces made me feel like I had one-hundred-and-fifty-one friends all looking forward to my birthday. Even the other students, who I knew were not as passionate about Pokémon as me, were enthused by the change in scenery and escape from the private school routine.

Witnessing Mom enter the classroom was jarring, as I had never seen more than one brown woman in the room since Grandma had dropped me off. But the power dynamic developing between parent and teacher did not interest me as much as the birthday cake in their hands, soon laid before my classmates and me, excited to eat anything but cafeteria food. The sole flame atop the number "6" shined in the dark room, and, remembering the ritual from the previous year's birthday, I made a silent wish before blowing it out.

Like all the wishes I have ever made, it was a sentiment rather than a clearly expressed thought. I wanted to be whole. I wanted to be understood. I wanted to be free from restraint. But little did I know that the institution in which I stood caused these suppressed feelings in the first place. But I would soon begin to know, as proven by Mr. Lopez's entrance into the classroom just minutes later.

As the no-nonsense, head principal of the school, Mr. Lopez enjoyed making routine visits to the classrooms to remind everyone that he mattered in a school of less than one hundred students. In contrast to the pastors, Mr. Lopez visited us to investigate and gather data rather than enjoy the company of his students. His balding scalp and wide-rimmed glasses became the symbol of insincerity to my young subconscious. Despite his brown skin, I held an unexplainable distrust toward him. He was different than Mom, Grandma, and Mrs. B. His brownness seemed to denote something else entirely.

He smiled like always, congratulating me on my recent grades and granting me blessed wishes. But throughout the entire affair he appeared uneasy and stiff, as if he had walked into a lion's den. Mom and Mrs. B continued laughing and enjoying the party, but Mr. Lopez seemed busy calculating his next move. Suppression was the name of the game played by the administration, and Pokémon became their next target. The next day, I brought my newly acquired Pokémon cards to class to show my classmates. A visibly distraught Mrs. B saw the cards and pulled me aside.

"We can't have those cards out in class, okay?"

I understood, so I waited until recess. But not even the swings could protect me from Mrs. B's gaze. She called me inside early.

"You can't bring those cards to school anymore."

Instinctively, I rebelled, questioning with innumerable whys until Mrs. B seemed to blurt out what she had been holding inside all day.

"Pokémon is the devil!"

Even as a young boy, I knew nonsense when I heard it. I had watched the first season at least twice over, and I knew that the television show emphasized the importance of friendship, following lofty dreams, and never giving up. And no one could prove that the video games and cards were inherently evil. What was evil? What was good? According to Mrs. B, the one thing I loved was "the devil" and therefore unacceptable for any good Christian.

Nearly in tears, I pocketed the cards and returned to the empty classroom, staring at the blank chalkboard. I imagined Aunt Aurora's red pick-up truck busting through the concrete walls, whisking me home where my Gameboy Color and Pokémon games awaited. I sat still in my seat for five minutes. No energy left to protest or play. So, I prayed.

In the black hole formed by my closed eyes and concentrated brain, I envisioned myself rising toward a flat, red surface that I knew for certain upheld the words that I had been searching for all this time — the words that would prove Mrs. B wrong and the Bible illustrations wrong and my skin color conceptions wrong. Religion, race, color — the fundamental words for that endeavor — were nowhere in my vocabulary. Perhaps they would emerge as I passed that surface, the ceiling of my mind, where all the answers lay.

Soon my classmates returned, and Mrs. B took the opportunity to make an announcement.

"Class, we can't have any more Pokémon in the classroom. Mr. Lopez says it's against the rules."

"Eek! Pokémon's the devil!" Kyle said with a hint of ironic sarcasm. He grinned at me.

Now that the idea had spread, I knew I had to stop it.

"It's not fair," I said.

The entire class stared at me before slipping back into the private school routine, silent and obedient.

By the end of the week, a parent-teacher conference had been scheduled with Mr. Lopez and Pastor Meyer as the guest stars. Mom, unaccustomed to these formal meetings, felt as uncomfortable as I did sitting in the principal's office, his detention paddle just inches away.

"Well, you see, it's school rules not to allow Pokémon on campus," Mr. Lopez said in a confident tone.

"Where does it say that?" Mom said, knowing from her own wallet that the nationwide craze had just begun.

Befuddled, Mr. Lopez bit his cheek and looked at Mrs. B, who chose to remain silent throughout the meeting.

"Well, I'll put it bluntly," Pastor Meyer said. "You know Pokémon originated in Japan, correct?"

Mom looked to me for assurance, and I proudly nodded my head.

"Well, as you know, the Japanese don't believe in god."

Suddenly, Mom began to laugh, and I imitated her. Mrs. B just sat there, listening and waiting until Pastor Meyer chimed in again.

"It's true. They have their own gods and beliefs. They believe in the devil and that he's hidden inside all things, like this pen. Look, the Japanese have backwards beliefs. Pokémon is a perfect example. You have kids going around catching these creatures to kill each other with, just like a typical Japanese. It can't be trusted or allowed in this school."

The urge to speak against Pastor Meyer arose in my chest in the form of increased heartbeats and an unexplainable anger. I wanted to prove him wrong. I wanted to prove that Pokémon had taught me more about life than anything the church's sermons had. But Mom responded in a flurry of words, furious and scathing. I fail to remember them all because of how scared I felt at that moment.

"I understand, but since the school's establishment, I've been an ardent supporter of god and proud of being Mexican," Mr. Lopez said. "We just think differently from the Japanese, that's all."

Infuriated, Mom took my hand and stormed out of the office. I drove home that day in her green Firebird. When we parked, I knew school would never be the same.

After attempting to overhear Mom and Grandma's secret kitchen table conversation, I was finally called to the center seat. A half-hour talk about morality and doing good and respect and equality ensued. Although I had never heard most of these words before, I felt I already knew about them from school. I kept nodding my head, staring out the window by the sink, wondering when I could go outside and play.

Despite Mr. Lopez's strict rules, I still traded Pokémon cards in the boy's bathroom. The 1st and 2nd graders were natural rebels, and I enjoyed simultaneously updating my collection and helping others do so as well. Throughout these ten-minute bathroom breaks, the thought that Mrs. B knew exactly what I was doing crept through the back of my mind, but it did not bother me. In fact, I was more than sure she knew. But since our meeting with Mr. Lopez and Pastor Meyer, she was visibly different. She seemed to passively resist against the racial prejudice she witnessed firsthand by allowing the card-trading to continue, and it affected her teaching. Gone were the eight-hour-smiles and jovial tones of voice. When Mrs. B became exhausted, she let it show unabashedly, especially during the random principal and pastor visits.

Even during prayer time, she appeared conflicted and concerned with an inner turmoil that not even god could solve. It was evident in her distracted mind, the forgotten and skipped words, the forcefulness of that final "Amen!" Soon I began skipping prayer, and then I saw the true pain in Mrs. B's face: the wrinkled forehead, the scrunched brow, the pained expression. But, like most six-year-olds, I paid it no mind until much later, when the events of childhood began to form a pile of unconscious thoughts and experiences that would shape the rest of my life.

As I grew older, my conflicts with attending a Christian school despite not holding Christian beliefs took their toll on my mind. I often dreamed about the possibility of escaping from an enclosed space, such as a cage placed in the middle of a forest or an airplane about to crash into the Gulf of Mexico. Often, a divine and omnipresent force prevented me from gaining true freedom. Then the dreams became nightmares of endless terrors that I later found to be manifestations of those kindergarten memories: Pastor Meyer's black wallet, Mr. Lopez's paddle. Whether it contained a floating, gigantic wallet that picked me up and placed me back in the cage or a possessed piece of wood following me, my dream-space was not a safe space.

The most unusual dream involved me becoming Japanese, but the weirdest part was never knowing it was the Japanese dream until I saw a river and stared at my reflection in it. The Rio Grande was the only river I knew at the time, although I had only seen it once. I remember it made a lasting impression on me because Mom said something about rivers changing all the time. Every time you looked into it, it wouldn't be the same river and you wouldn't be the same person either. I don't know why my brain interpreted that as turning Japanese. All I cared about during the dream was what would Mr. Lopez say? Could I go to school? How would my classmates treat me? Every time I woke up, I was thankful that I was born a white Mexican. But would I grow up to be a nice Mexican like Mom and Grandma, or a mean Mexican like Mr. Lopez? Or a white bully like Pastor Meyer? At least I could choose.

Mrs. B quit after I finished the 2nd grade. The motions of attending sermons and memorizing Bible verses and praising god had become commonplace and soul-sucking to both of us. Although I did not enroll in a different school until the 6th grade, I had already realized I needed to escape. But until then, the issue of morality and spiritually concerned my Mom, who hated Faith Christian School but loved its religious curriculum. Receiving a Christian education was essential to her, even though the school was not accredited, and all graduates received a symbolic rock instead of a high school degree during graduation.

"But Mom," I said one day during a car ride. "If I went to public school, I could talk to real Christian Mexicans."

She tried to stop herself from laughing.

"Yeah, Mexicans who really, really believe in god," I said, clarifying. "And maybe there are some who don't. But at least I could play Pokémon with them."

The response triggered a laugh so hard that Mom had to pull over to catch her breath. Even the palm trees seemed to bend over in laughter. I laughed too, but for different reasons.

The words had come out. Not gracefully, not precisely, but they had come out. I had never felt more spiritually liberated than the day I could begin to express my suppressed frustration, anger, and disappointment in the botched version of Christianity taught at Faith Christian School. I spent the ride home looking at buildings and cars and people burn under the South Texas sun, feeling like they were new surroundings, although they had always been there.

(2018)

SCHOLARSHIP BOY

It started when I spoke Latin to some trokiando vatos. Under the Whataburger sign, a group of teens clicked their tongues at May and me, probably because she was morena and I was lugging *The Collected Works of F. Scott Fitzgerald* like a Bible. Pissed, I yelled, "Pinche pueri chingao!" They laughed in machismo.

In response, May clicked her tongue twice, exploding into a swarm of expletives so rich with Spanish flair I couldn't keep up: A bunch of Elber Galargas with vergas largas up their culos chulos. Catching the vatos off guard with the coveted este and puckering her lips with every pinche, her words whirled around the parking lot, injecting levity here and debasing their manhood there, leaving them all looking at each other with faces like "Awww!"

Only May could charm barrio boys into performing that joyful conceit. They knew nobody meant anybody harm, just good fun, move along. The vatos reverted to talking shit past each other until they peeled off.

"I read about this," I said, poking my temple too hard. "'Bye-lingualism,' losing words every day."

"You speak three languages," May said. "Your Spanish counts. Call it 'try-lingualism' instead. Maybe you'll 'pueri-vail.'"

After we ordered and sat down at a booth, we read sentences aloud until the breakfast crowd arrived. May would occasionally glance toward the window, watching construction workers eating on the back of trucks while teachers rushed past mouthing good morning, smiling. Everyone was going their own way and watching each other go, not knowing where anyone came from. Who knew that we had sat reciting prose since midnight, or that I could barely speak Spanish — and where would we go from here? We were all here along the border, but we were so far apart. Only May and I knew it was travel day, the Friday before fall semester started.

"Last time Mom picked me up from the airport, she spoke to me only in English. I could tell she had practiced," I said. "Then she pointed to these cars abandoned on the side of the expressway and said that I should write to the city about them. Because — she said this straight — I write like a güero, and people would listen."

"It's dumb, but she was trying to compliment you," May said. "Hey, don't let those guys get to you."

"No, I've been thinking about it," I said, May nodding with a half-knowing look. "I never knew the distance between us would hit so close to home."

"You can't expect her to know your Princeton world."

The weight of the word hit me like humidity seeping in through the door. It sounded foreign, like it didn't belong outside the Orange Bubble. You don't talk about paradise while talking about living in limbo, just like you don't speak Latin in the parking lot. And you don't act like a Princeton man when you're trying to be a borderlands man, two worlds scraping past each other into something worse than an Anzaldua open wound.

"I expected the distance, but it's when she tries to bridge that distance," I said. "The other day she told me she saw *The Great Gatsby*, that it was really good, but the book cover is better than the movie cover. The poster with este ¿como se llama? Leo. The book is always better, right? I said, yeah, you're right."

May leaned forward, staring at me until I held the book to my face. There was the paradox: Replacing my face with the cover, a hand-drawn Fitzgerald inside a portrait, was like fading into a future version of myself that wasn't real yet. And it would never really be real, but everyone would believe it's me. May pushed it away and poked my nose. Dangling her keys, she motioned to her red pick-up truck — time to move.

But all I could think about was the way Mom had asked the question — with that familiar, doubtful, final syllable that also escapes my mouth during class discussions — that I had let linger in the air for a minute, too tired to carry the illusion through. It was the most painful minute, watching her lips quiver in anticipation of some sign of acceptance from her only son. It was then I realized I had already left home and there was no return.

***

Did you tell her about PhDs? May texted me.

No. I'm gonna wait a year.

To tell her?!

No. To apply.

I ignored May's phone call and adjusted my eyes to Princeton in the dark, illuminated by light posts leading up the hill toward Nassau Street drenched in early winter rain. The raindrops had fallen so quietly I didn't hear them from inside the Mudd Manuscript Library. Away from researchers twice my age, I could breathe and think. Why Fitzgerald? Professor Benderson had asked. Because I want to become a writer like him. Why the archive? Because something's there. When I told him, I imagine it's like in the 8th grade when I went to the library and unexpectedly found a tattered copy of *This Side of Paradise* and my life was never the same, he laughed and shook his head.

And the jet-black winter followed me back inside, past the walls aligned with portraits of dignitaries looking down on the researchers sitting at tables, manuscripts and letters eschewed, who in turn stared at my footsteps squeaking all the way to my seat. The weight of gaze was ancient, as if I walked in steps already treaded, and lifting my pencil meant paving more of that path. But every word

I wrote floated past my eyes. In the middle of a sentence, my thoughts would break — it was time for Mom's insulin injection, so I texted the reminder to her — and returning to the work tinged every word with the chilling reminder of the distance between she and me.

I would never catch up. I was doomed to spend hours — years if I wasn't careful — thinking about everything that's already happened. That time a century ago, that place with writers so far removed from me. In a portrait on the far side of the room, I imagined Fitzgerald's face with eyes piercing me. That silent, moving mouth urging me to say something worth something — but what? All I had was a blank page with the moments lagging away.

Taking hold of a folder of letters, I spread them across the table and read them all. The writerly wit broke through, and soon the room fell away, bringing me face-to-face with Hemingway chastising Fitzgerald, "Forget your personal tragedy," the intensity of his vibrato resounding as if their voices merged in my head, two writers becoming one — *güero* writing at its finest — and the thought derailed me back to the Mudd Library. I packed and left.

I'm not ready. I texted May. *I have nothing academic to say.*

I stared at the screen so long I jumped at a message from Mom: a photo of the television from the living room couch with the message, *did the shot going to sleep.*

You don't need all the answers to go to graduate school, May texted back.

I don't need a PhD to become a writer.

But those stipends wouldn't hurt.

Walking along FitzRandolph Gate, I crunched the numbers. The Stanford stipend would allow me to send Mom two hundred dollars a month, and the Harvard fellowship would make it three hundred. She was already getting one hundred a month from my financial aid, so any net increase meant more insulin and doctor visits. The math rolled on, possibilities unraveled again and again all the way to Olive's, where I ordered dinner and remembered working on the other side of the deli counter back home — those afterschool rituals of ticking away at the register, fighting for more hours, numbing all the sensations around me — and never writing anything despite calling myself a writer. The possibility of working anywhere outside a university always shut down that dream. The mental bandwidth, the load of carrying all these ideas while at home, the work beast sucking up wages so I could pay bills and destress Mom. It was always a rat race toward more and more. There would never be enough to end it.

Whenever I visited, the man cutting the meats would glance toward me repeatedly. He always seemed open to talk, but he only spoke Spanish. I knew I would struggle to keep up past the first exchange. Along the border I could assume we were all Mexican, but here I couldn't pinpoint the nuances in accents to know if I was speaking to anyone else in the Latino world. Maybe he thought the same of me; a white man who knows little Spanish must not be from that world. I wish I could tell him about the border, my trips to

Reynosa on the three-day weekends to spend time with extended family. There must be stories in our heads that could bridge the gap between us, but I couldn't get them out. In the end, it was just picking up a sandwich, but it felt like a test. I always left Olive's with a big smile and one too many gracias.

Up Witherspoon Street, I watched a professor and student gesticulating in the distance. They walked from Nassau Hall with a brisk gait, the same energy I felt walking into Fitzgerald's old eating club. The spirits of the dead circling inside their brains, from Pompey to Proust. When the man departed, I realized it was Professor Benderson. The student's gaze followed his tweed coat dipping through the crowds, disappearing past me without acknowledging me. And I witnessed the moment the haunting loneliness hit both of us, two aspiring young men craving validation from bespectacled elders. The student jerked his head down, and he shambled through the campus for another marathon of reading and writing. I imagined he too strived for that moment where the words would come naturally. Where hands become weightless, and the body simply moves along with the rhythm and the mind suppresses the thought: What are you doing really?

"Professor Benderson," I said, half-hoping he wouldn't hear. He did.

He turned and registered my face and name for a moment and smiled.

"Fitzgerald, the crack-up," he said. "How goes it in the archives?"

"It's like I'm a different person in there. Like not everyone can see these documents, so it's like — reading the original handwriting grants me insights into Fitzgerald's state of mind during his writing processes. He was an infamous drunk, so —"

"Yes, yes. Let's set a deadline for the next chapter. End of next week? Yes."

And with a reluctant wave, he crossed Nassau Street and disappeared into the crowds of townies and tourists. Off to read, maybe to write, as if time was running out. At least that's what I imagined professors did all day. Sauntering is for students and scuttling is for scholars.

Occasionally, while typing Professor Benderson's every word in lecture, I would remember that I was sitting in Princeton, the place I had spent four years acing classes to arrive on a full scholarship. Glancing at my classmates' faces brought no smiles nor reflections of any kind, but their stone-faced stares toward the lectern would remind me how we had all arrived, although differently. That made the bustle of post-lecture exciting. Ruminating over the professor's parting ideas in our minds, we set off to the next scheduled thing, wandering in the autumn air having forgotten where we came from because we knew where we were now. We knew every path led to FitzRandolph Gate on graduation day.

I walked past the gate and onto campus as the sun set. Princeton glowed golden with every lamppost standing tall against the breezy dusk. Through the haze of students rushing to the Rocky dining hall ordained in fancy wood I couldn't name, I felt the vitality of the place — sensing that people like Fitzgerald came before me as I walked with spirits, realizing my body had lifted out of the barrio and into paradise. Into Frist Campus Center I drifted, my subconscious drawing me toward the spirits on the walls: Ralph Nader, Toni Morrison, so many towering Princeton figures with quotes plastered onto the bricks, shadows of ideas infused into the structures. I stood in the corner, staring at Fitzgerald's:

"It was always the becoming he dreamed of, never the being."

After months of procrastinating graduate school applications, I found my opening: "I will work hard in any place that gives me the space to become."

***

Hey handsome

You're drunk, May.

Did you party hardy last night

It's thesis week.

iTs tHeSiS wEeK

So your semester's done?

What makes you say that, Princeton

Because you're drunk on a Sunday.

Well the good thing about this school is I can do all my homework and all my booze in one day

Community college sounding nice now.

Don't patron me haha

And your parents?

The court days were set last week

Any idea when it's all done?

When the judge says

Well, are they staying home?

Yeah, except for H-E-B

There's delivery now online so they don't have to drive.

I know

I take it you drive them too.

No

Ok

Just imagine how phucked up that would be over missing a stop sign or something

Yeah, that is fucked.

I hope that never happens

The paperwork takes time, but it's worth it.

That's why I stayed not because of the booze

I know.

Do you ever wonder

No, I understand it's hard.

what's it like to stop walking and say wow I'm here

It's a dream to be here.

Yeah but how

How what?

How is it to feel that

It feels good. It makes me work harder. Like if I were somewhere else, I wouldn't feel the same pressure to go the extra mile.

Isn't that weird how a place does that

Yeah, I guess so.

***

Graduation day smelled like hoagies. I met Mom at the Dinky station, imprinted on her face the same expression on my freshman face four years ago. Her open smile widened even as she dedicated her first Princeton experience to walking through the WaWa and observing the superiority of their snack assortment. This is better than my own store's, she repeated. In and out students went, snacks in hand, wandering around Whitman College with robes swishing in the mid-afternoon light before stopping to pose for legacy photos with parents and grandparents. Mom and I walked through campus silently.

"No wonder you like being here so much," she said, pointing to McCosh Hall. It was one of those half-thoughts I preferred to leave alone.

Standing beside Mom in the McCosh courtyard was unsettling. She had always been of the border, and to see her here collided what I felt was precious about home with what I admired about college. It was almost tempting to feel like we had both accomplished something significant by merely standing here. In every direction, families mingled with ease, blending into the place as if posing for the admissions pamphlets. That ease had often unnerved me, and I saw Mom struggle with it too, that sense of knowing our belonging to this place was different. Just different. Maybe it was the other families' comfortable laughter that did it, or how they could stroll the campus with shoes worth more than my wardrobe. She and I exchanged a look of knowing.

We followed the crowd of parents and students funneling into McCosh Hall to sit in a lecture room with the wooden desks too small for anyone. Several English professors sat on foldable chairs on the stage while others were interspersed before them, mingling before the award ceremony. Former classmates stood to become recognized for their abnormally high GPAs and intensive senior thesis research. That familiar grin of self-satisfaction and obligatory humbleness pained every face, with a few tinges of a top-of-the-world gladness reminiscent of kindergarten graduation. I don't know how I looked when my name was called, but I know I read the certificate twice to ensure I did receive two awards — one for creative writing and another for my senior thesis on Fitzgerald — before Professor Benderson rose to shake my hand.

The grip reminded me of the days reading short stories sentence-by-sentence in his office hours, commenting on diction and themes, dragging my brain across the track of literary analysis so I could prove to Professor Benderson that I knew I could do it like the well-read student he considered me. His reminder that I was headed to Los Angeles for graduate school reassured me that I knew where I was going — even if I didn't know how to get there yet.

After the ceremony, Mom and I looked for Professor Benderson during the English Department's outdoor party. Near the chapel, he stood alone with hands in his pockets. If I weren't his student, I would have assumed him a townie amused by this annual ritual that sent students out the gates and into the world. He leaned as if unused to leaning, as if expecting something to break his uncomfortable posture. I recognized the perpetual wallflower feeling.

"Professor, this is my mother," I said, my voice deeper than usual.

"How do you like it here at Princeton?" Mom asked, looking him in the eyes.

"Well, you always like the place you're currently at."

A brief silence, and I worried that's all that would be said between the two figureheads of the two worlds I straddled. Then the familiar convenience-store jovialities Mom had mastered her whole adult life came forward, surprisingly to the relief of Professor Benderson, whose shoulders relaxed at Mom placing her hand on his arm like a lifelong friend.

"He's headed to Los Angeles in the fall," Mom said with hints of confusion in her voice. "I never understood that. Five more years of school. ¡Acaba de terminar cuatro aquí! Otra vez."

"Well, now he's on his way to becoming un erudito," Professor Benderson said with a wide grin.

"Becoming? Well, he acts like one already with all the fancy books he talks about!"

Becoming — it hadn't hit me yet. For half an hour we spoke about Pharr and Princeton, labor and research, hunger and abundance as if we knew all each other. As if Mom and Professor Benderson had met sometime in a past life and knew what to say and how to say it. I knew this transitory moment would mean something more in the future, but I still enjoyed it while it lasted.

***

The weekend was full of festivities and ceremonies that made me feel like something was beginning. The days were long, but only because I didn't want them to end. It was traveling day again — this time back home. For days, Mom had spoken of a surprise that would "hit you hard before we leave." I thought it was the gift she brought with her on the plane and what I decided to carry with me that last weekend on campus: the same paperback version of *This Side of Paradise* I had found in the 8th grade. It probably made me seem sentimental to my peers, but the touch of the book reminded me of where I had come from and where I was now.

But it wasn't the book. With all my bags packed and dragged to north campus, I was ready to hail a ride to the airport with Mom until she told me to turn around. On the curb outside East Pyne Hall was a red pick-up truck parked illegally. It honked obnoxiously loud when I first saw it. May lowered the window and yelled equally as loud: road trip.

With a look that betrayed all the worry in her chest, Mom hugged me.

"I'll see you in a few days. Enjoy it. And be careful."

"I'll take care of him," May said, hands cupped around her mouth with her tongue sticking out. As I approached the truck, she settled into the driver's seat with a self-satisfied smile. When she looked up at me again, I felt like she was looking past me. At the trees exploding with green, at the castles in the sky, at Princeton. Her Princeton, a place unlike anyone else's.

Just when I was about to say something I thought sounded insightful, May reached into the passenger seat and threw a paperback at me. *On the Road* by Jack Kerouac.

"We're headed to Mexico, Sal," May said, revving the engine. "So, we can get you reading books written by Mexicans."

"I don't have a passport," I said, feigning concern.

"Okay, okay. The river, then. We'll take a dip and then turn back. Ever seen *Stand and Deliver*? When they jump in the ocean... like that."

We laughed, ready to go. It was summer, and the future was still ours.

(2020)

ABOUT THE AUTHOR

Thomas Ray Garcia is a writer, educator, and entrepreneur from Pharr, Texas. At Princeton University, he received the Ward Mathis Short Story Prize for his U.S.-Mexico borderlands fiction. The River Runs: Stories, winner of the Américo Paredes Literary Arts Prize for Fiction, is his first book. Thomas is also the founder and executive director of the College Scholarship Leadership Access Program (CSLAP), a 501(c)(3) nonprofit focused on increasing college enrollment and graduation rates in South Texas. His website is www.thomasraygarcia.com

www.ingramcontent.com/pod-product-compliance
Lightning Source LLC
Chambersburg PA
CBHW050349030726
47503CB00008B/2692